THE NAMELESS

Task Force Zombie, Book 1

WILLIAM ALAN WEBB

δ

Dingbat Publishing
Humble, Texas

TASK FORCE ZOMBIE: THE NAMELESS
Copyright © 2019 by William Alan Webb
Primary Print ISBN 978-1-659305234

Published by Dingbat Publishing
Humble, Texas

We will send him the sons whom our wives have nursed,
Were death to follow, mine own the first.
Better by far they there should die
Than be driven all from our land to fly,
Flung to dishonor and beggary.

From "The Song of Roland"

FOREWORD

If this is your first introduction to the world of **The Last Brigade,** then let me start by thanking you for your trust in me. There is a compact between a writer and his or her readers, an agreement that, in return for the reader's investment in the writer, the author will tell the best story of which they are capable. In other words, they won't mail it in just because they know some people will buy it because they wrote it.

I never, ever take this for granted. Whether you like my books or hate them (I prefer that you like them), I want you to understand that I will always give you the best I've got. My success occurred later in life than it does for most people, especially writers. It means that I do not now, nor will I ever, feel entitled to your loyalty.

Okay, enough with the mawkish sentimentality.

The world of **The Last Brigade** sprang fully formed in my mind; having said that, it doesn't mean that I realized all the stories, characters or villains, that would crawl out of the locked closets in my brain to demand space in the series. The whole thing started with Nick the A standing on the ramparts of the Hohensalzburg, at which point I didn't even know his name. Some people have questioned naming him Angriff, since that is the German word for attack, and I suppose a case could be made that I should have used *Angreifer*, meaning attacker. But people who think that nobody would ever be named either one of those are ignoring the surname Krieger, since *krieg* is the German word for war and *Krieger* means warrior. Warrior and attacker aren't so very different. Moreover, the family was given the honorific surname Angriff during the Thirty Years' War by nobody less than the King of Bavaria himself, as will be seen in an upcoming story titled *The Moles of Vienna*.

For those who haven't read that original draft of Nick in Salzburg, which is vastly different from the way it wound up in *Standing The Final Watch*, it is reproduced in its entirety in the book that details how it all happened, *Unsuck Your Book, 8 Months from First Draft to the Promised Land*.

Green Ghost came along pretty early in the process. His name pays homage to John Ringo's main character in *Ghost*. Reading that book was a pivotal moment for me, not so much because it's great literature, but because it was the final step in shaking off the mental shackles installed in me when I majored in creative writing. Ringo's book was fun! I give my education credit for teaching me how to form sentences, how to realize a bad sentence from a good, etc. BUT... my training was in how to write literary fiction, not in how to write books people wanted to read.

Literary fiction depends far more on character and setting than on plot. In many cases, it's hard to even find a plot, and anything related to a genre was unwelcome in the classroom. Now, some people can pull off concentrating on details and characters while writing amazing books. Not many and most who try cannot, but a few succeed. I wasn't one of them. What *Ghost* gave me permission to do was to write a book that I would enjoy reading, a book that allowed for over-the-top characters . And believe me when I tell you that I have never enjoyed writing anything more than I did *Standing The Final Watch.*

So here we are at a place I never dreamed we'd be, circling back to fill in some blanks that were necessarily left out of **The Last Brigade.** I've taken a little heat because US Special Ops teams don't operate the way Task Force Zombie does, although in those books I've alluded to why that happened. But I felt compelled to explain in detail because I think it's a good story. And for the careful reader, here's a nugget: the Stingers that are at the core of this story also show up in **The Last Brigade.**

Lastly, I look at these author forewords as a way to catch up with readers I haven't had a chance to meet in person or online, and who aren't subscribed to my newsletter at www.thelastbrigade.com. Kind of like the Christmas letter that people send out to catch their friends and relatives up on what happened during the year. But like those letters, there's a point where they became too long, and I'm there.

Until next time!

Bill Webb
December 3, 2019

"The right individual, in the right place at the right time, can change the course of human history."
Lieutenant General Nicholas T. Angriff

Camp Zippo, 5 miles west of Yoboki, Djibouti
0712 hours, July 12, 2012

Without realizing he was doing it, Major General Norm Fleming rose up and rolled his buttocks from side to side. The muscles in his lower back ached from sinking into the worn-out couch. For the third or fourth time, he scooted forward to the edge, elbows on knees and hands clasped as he stared at the wall.

The clarity of the one-hundred-inch flat screen monitor mounted there was enough to count the hairs on the rats that scurried for cover as the running man's footfalls scuffed the concrete alley, where the rats had been gnawing through a pile of garbage. The three high-ranking officers in the room saw this because a UAV circled Mogadishu at 2,000 feet, its long-range, high-definition camera focused on a man sprinting through back alleys with eight or ten others in close pursuit. Hurdling over a spilled crate of rotting tomatoes without breaking stride, he ducked as bullets tore into one of the alley's cinder block walls.

White robes flapped behind his pursuers, all of whom ran after him carrying what looked like AK-47s. That made following them among the knots of peddlers and tent covers lining the alley easy, since most men wore jeans and t-shirts. But instead of either white or jeans, the running man wore the mottled green, dark brown, and pinkish khaki camouflage uniform of *Spetsnaz*, with a black knit toboggan covering his face. All three people in the room recognized the rifle he carried in one hand as the Russian AKM, a modernized version of the AK-47, with a grenade launcher attached.

"What's his name?" Nick Angriff said. Fleming wasn't fooled by the dispassion in his voice. He knew his friend too well, but even had he not, the words didn't match the obvious worry in Angriff's taut features, or the involuntary clenching and unclenching of his hands.

Fleming turned to the third person in the room, a short, heavy-set major named Kamiya Jones, who stood beside them. She sensed him looking at her and flicked her eyes from the screen to his face. Fleming's lifted left eyebrow showed they awaited the answer to Angriff's question.

"Well, Major?"

"Green Ghost, sir," Jones said, trying to sound confident. Fleming assumed her nervousness came from having Nick the A drop in to watch the op happening live. That was enough to make anybody nervous. "That's all we know, per your instructions. All secrecy protocols have been followed to the letter."

Various shades of brown danced across Angriff's eyeballs as reflections from the screen played across them like a movie screen. He stared at the monitor with a fixation close to hypnosis. "He's good. Fast and agile. I hope to God he survives."

"He got his target."

"I know."

"You thought he'd abort."

"But he didn't. That either makes him dedicated or stupid. I'm praying it's the first one."

"Even if nobody gets out, the HVT was worth it."

"I hate that kind of math. We're already down three First Team operatives, not to mention three damned heroic Americans."

Fleming half-smiled and nodded at the archaic sounding plaudit. Most politicians, civilian or military, no longer used terms like *heroic*, considering it too politically incorrect in an era when you couldn't call a terrorist a terrorist, but had to call them insurgents instead. But Nick Angriff didn't give a damn about what anybody else thought about his patriots; to him, a hero was a hero, a patriot was a patriot, and a terrorist was a terrorist.

The running man turned down a street filled with food vendor carts and milling crowds of women wearing burkhas, shopping for the evening meal. Four men followed him into the mass of humanity. Puffs of smoke trailed from the muzzles of their AK-47s, and the people on the street running for cover showed the watchers that they were shooting at the man they chased. A stocky woman clad head to toe in black fell to the ground and didn't move.

At the other end of the short street, two more white-robed men knelt and opened up, catching the lone gunmen in a deadly crossfire. Like most such militias, their aim was indiscriminate. Fire discipline to them meant shoot and keep shooting until you run out of ammo.

"Damn," Angriff said. "They've got him trapped."

"The QRT can't go in without compromising our role in this one."

Angriff exhaled through his nostrils in the way that told Fleming he was upset. "I know."

"And we can't use drones for the same reason."

"I wrote the ROEs for this mission, remember?"

As they watched, two more women toppled when strays ripped into the crowd. The stream of bullets hit the paving stones and alley walls around Green Ghost as he kept running straight at the two men. At the moment they converged on him, he made an impossible leap sidewise, tucked the AKM into his chest, and dove forward. Landing on his right shoulder, he rolled into a kneeling position, brought the rifle up, and hosed both men with a long burst. Red splotches appeared all over the white robes and they were dead before they fell.

Fleming felt his mouth hanging open at what should have been an impossible feat, and saw both Angriff and Major Jones doing the same. Such acrobatics belonged at the Olympics, or in Las Vegas.

The four men fifty feet behind now had a clear field of fire, but by the time they'd retargeted on him, he was gone behind a food stall. Two children cowered in the shadows near the alley wall, their dead mother lying at their feet.

Green Ghost saw his chance.

The militiamen advanced in line abreast, cautiously stepping over bodies and bicycles and broken food carts. Smashed tomatoes made the paving stones slippery. When a screaming woman staggered down the street, unseen under her black burkha, they paid her no mind but went on searching for the assassin of their patron. The wailing woman leaned against an alley wall as they walked past, her face in her hands.

It was only when 7.62 millimeter rounds tore into their backs that they realized what had happened to the assassin. One managed to turn halfway around before a bullet severed his spine, but the rest all died facing the wrong way.

"Get him out of there, Major," Angriff said. "Whatever it takes, get him out. I'll take any heat on this."

"You know the—" Fleming started, before Angriff cut him off.

"Yes, I know the blowback."

"He's the one?"

"If he's not, then nobody is. Get him home in one piece, Major Jones."

#

CHAPTER 2

*"Leadership is the art of getting someone else to do
something you want done because he wants to do it."*
General Dwight D. Eisenhower

Camp Zippo, Djibouti
1433 hours, July 14, 2012

Nick Angriff didn't know who'd designed the
Portable Command Center, the PCC, but whoever it
was, he owed them a bottle of their finest favorite
drink. He'd been told that in the future such shel-
ters would be made by 3-D printers, whatever the
hell those were, but that was then and this was
now. The outside temperature routinely soared past
100 degrees Fahrenheit, even with the afternoon
shade cast by the peak of the mountain under
whose eaves they'd established the temporary headquarters. Angriff prided himself on being a tough
soldier, but the PCC had a very effective air-
conditioning system and nothing said you couldn't
be both tough and comfortable.

Lunch had been a barbeque beef MRE that
wasn't half bad. He opened the humidor on the left
side of his desk and pulled out a cigar, a Cubana
Monte Cristo Especiales Number Three. His after-
lunch ritual involved toasting the foot and spending
twenty minutes enjoying the smoke, despite a dozen

Army regulations against doing such a thing, but not today. Today he was going to ask a man to do something he'd never before asked anyone to do — give up not just his identity, but his entire life. The cigar would only be a prop.

After a knock on his office door, Angriff told the corporal on duty to bring in his visitor. The man who entered stood six feet tall, with a lean build and face, but an expression that Angriff found hard to read. *Was that a smirk?* No, he decided, not a smirk, just extreme confidence. He was the best of the best Special Forces operators in the American armed forces and such people by definition could not be intimidated. Although he only took four steps to reach Angriff's desk, the man's gait had a predatory stalk to it.

He wore regulation ACUs with no insignia, awards, or name. The man stopped three feet in front of Angriff's desk and came to attention. "Reporting as ordered, sir."

"At ease."

Angriff sensed something different about the younger man's rigid stance, even when standing at ease. His weight seemed balanced so he could move in any direction, which was something the general had rarely seen in men other than himself. It took years of training to perfect, unless... unless you were born with it. Few men were.

"Smoke 'em if you've got 'em," he said in his most comradely tone.

The man barely lifted one eyebrow. Most people wouldn't have noticed, but Angriff did. He had the same tell-tale gesture.

"I don't smoke, sir."

"That's good. It's a nasty habit, although a fine

cigar every now and then never hurt anybody."

The man didn't respond, but only kept his gaze fixed straight ahead at the photo of George Patton behind the desk. Although he wore no rank insignia, Angriff knew he was a first lieutenant, and like any first lieutenant with half a brain, he obviously knew that when facing a three-star general it was best to say as little as possible.

After a few seconds, Angriff made a downward waving motion. "Have a seat, son."

That snapped the man's head around. His eyes squinted ever so slightly, as if trying to figure out what Angriff's words meant. Then, awkwardly, he pulled the folding chair close to the center of the desktop and sat, back straight, legs at perfect right angles to the knees.

"A.C. feels good, doesn't it? All the way out here in the middle of Hell?"

"Yes, sir. It does."

"Do you know why you're here? Or the reason for all of the security protocols?"

Once again the man's blue eyes narrowed. Angriff noticed it as a *tell* and knew he was thinking about how to answer. He'd been a lieutenant once, too, but never alone in the office of a three-star general — just his angry battalion C.O, a bird colonel. That had been frightening enough.

"It has not been explained to me, sir."

"Then you must be wondering what the hell this is about, or why I haven't used your rank title yet. We'll get to that, but first, you've doubtless heard stories about me, and now here you are. Let me make you feel better; you're not here because you've done something wrong, you're here because you've done a lot of things right. So here's what I want you to do. I want you to relax and forget my rank, if you can. At least during this interview. I need a sense of who you are, so I need you to be yourself. Can you do that for me, son?"

For the third time the man squinted, as if solving a puzzle. Angriff decided that he would have to speak to the lieutenant about that. Obvious *tells* were a bad thing in the world of black ops.

"I can try, sir," the younger man said.

"I don't want you to try. I want you to do it."

Their eyes locked for a second and the man nodded once.

"Done, sir."

"And that goes for sirs, too. There's nobody here but me and you."

"Roger that."

"So here's what I know about you. You hold the rank of O-1, you're 23 years old, and you qualified for Delta One. Your athleticism is off the charts, literally. Physical skills in the top one-tenth of one percent, hand-eye coordination superb, speed and reflexes like a hummingbird. You shoot, on the run and one-handed, like the gun is an extension of your body. How am I doing so far?"

The man hesitated, but this time he didn't squint. Could he be learning to expunge that bad habit all by himself?

"Say it," Angriff continued. "You won't piss me off, not right now, anyway. Go on, say it."

"I'm not sure I'm as good as you think I am."

"No?"

"No."

"So the officers who wrote your OERs are... what? Incompetent? Full of shit? Or are you really the most physically gifted son of a bitch in this man's army, but think it's somehow dishonorable to say so?"

The younger man didn't squint, didn't even blink. "I'm one of them."

"Good." Angriff nodded and leaned forward on his elbows. He picked up the cigar so the scent of the tobacco would be closer to his nostrils. "You know what else I know about you? Not much, except that when the mission is important enough, you're willing to die to complete it, even if it's alone."

"You mean Mogadishu?"

"Unless there's another time I don't know about, yes. I watched a lot of that mission, live. I'm the one who ordered the pickup team to go in and get you. Extraction under combat conditions isn't something a lot of officers want to risk, so I made it clear that it was on my responsibility. I don't usually like to jump the chain of command, but this was an exception."

"General, may I speak bluntly?"

"I wish you would."

"What is this about?"

"From this point forward, everything we talk about is top secret. You will not discuss this with anyone. Is that understood?"

"Yes, sir." His clenched jaws made it obvious he wanted to say more, but junior officers didn't question generals. Angriff liked that he wanted to ask, but didn't.

"The truth is that it's Above Top Secret. Less than ten people in the world know what we're about to discuss. Any leaks traced to you will mean an immediate court-martial on charges of treason. But this is a volunteer assignment and I want you to fully understand the ramifications of your actions."

"I get it," he said, with the barest hint of impatience.

"Very well. I like you, you kind of remind me of me, when I was your age." Once again the man cocked his head. "Why do you keep doing that, Lieutenant?"

"Sir? I mean, do what?"

"You tilted your head like my German shepherd used to do. Why?"

"I'm sorry. It won't happen again."

That didn't answer his question, but Angriff let it go. Another *tell*?

Leaning forward, elbows on his desk, he laid aside the cigar and clasped his hands together. "When those SEALs got bin Laden last year, a lot of people back home thought that was it, the War on Terror was over. No matter how many times you warn them the end's not even in sight, they're getting tired of this endless commitment. I don't blame them either. We've been at this for eleven years and nobody can say how much longer it'll last, or if it might spread. I personally think we'll be in Syria before it's all over, and probably Iran, too. But that's not what the American public wants to hear.

"But something else they don't want to hear about is America meddling in other countries, and especially not American Special Forces conducting what the public thinks of as black ops. Under the current Rules of Engagement, we can't kill until they shoot at us first, and sometimes not even then. All too often our hands are tied. That's why it sometimes takes so long to get a mission authorized, and why you sometimes miss a target because of the delay. Nobody wants to take the responsibility if something goes wrong. I know the teams hate it, but that's how it is. Are you with me so far?"

"Yes, sir."

"Remember, no sirs? We're just having a conversation."

"If you say so, General."

"I do. Because of the political situation in the world today, and especially in North Africa and the Middle East, the president has put severe restrictions on the use of Special Forces, and as he's the commander-in-chief, we are duty-bound to obey his orders. There are two reasons for this decision. First, so that America can't be blamed if something goes wrong, and second, because there are a lot of people who believe drones and robotic weapons are the way of the future. Don't get me wrong, if I can send a machine into combat instead of a man, I'll do it every time. But there are some missions that a drone simply can't do. And that's our current dilemma — there are missions we need to perform using flesh and blood, but we cannot risk having them go sideways and be tracked back to the U.S. That's where you come in."

"You mean all the security, code names, and stuff?"

"That's what I mean. I'm organizing a new top level unit to go after the people our regular forces can't. Members of this unit will still be members of our armed forces. Each man, or woman — the nature of this unit will call for more than just physical combat prowess — every member will be raised one rank—"

"Permanently?" the man blurted, before realizing he'd interrupted a three–star general. Generals were gods, and a three-star general was like the God of War. "I'm sorry."

Angriff's swivel chair squeaked as he leaned

back. "If there was anybody here but us two, I'd have your ass for interrupting me—"

"It won't happen again, sir."

"—but there's not anybody else here," Angriff went on, as if the man hadn't spoken. "And I told you to speak freely, so as long as we're alone, you do that. Clear?"

The younger man didn't stammer when he replied. To Angriff, he didn't even seem nervous, just... wary? "Yes, sir. Clear."

"And for the last time, drop the sirs!"

"Got it."

"Good. To answer your question, yes, all promotions will be permanent. You, for example, would be elevated to OF-2. And because of the extraordinary sacrifices that will be asked of you, your pay will be raised one grade beyond *that*, so you'd be paid as a major."

"I can speak freely?"

"You can."

"Okay... what's the catch?"

"I'd heard you were smart, that you can see to the heart of things quicker than most people. That's why you're sitting in my office. As you guessed, there *is* a catch, and it's a big one."

Angriff laid it all out for him, holding nothing back. The new unit would get dangerous missions in places usually beyond support by the American military. They would be anonymous, wear non-regulation clothing, no insignia and no rank designations. If they died in action, whenever possible they would receive a service funeral with burial in a national cemetery, perhaps even Arlington if they qualified, although that had been tightened a lot as the land filled up with American heroes. Probably the worst of it was losing their identity. They would only be known by code names, even to each other. "That's why I don't know anything about you other than rank and service branch."

When he'd finished, the man paused a moment to let the implications sink in. "Are you asking me to join this new unit, General?"

"Join it? Hell, I want you to lead it."

The American compound was small, as it had to be. Although Djibouti was a stout American ally, not everybody was happy about that fact. Like in all Muslim countries, there was a jihadist element that only wanted to kill the infidels. There was no reason to advertise an American army base out in the western desert.

Several people had joined them at Angriff's invitation, using up every chair in his little office and straining the air-conditioning to cool the room. The lieutenant stood until Angriff motioned him to sit down again. He made the introductions while a corporal brought in a pot of coffee and some foam cups, and then left after filling one for each man.

"Lieutenant, allow me to introduce Major Kordibowski and Major General Fleming. General Fleming is second in command of the Combined Joint Task Force, Horn of Africa, at Camp Lemmonier." *U.S. Africa Command, USAC.*

"I'm familiar with it, sir." For the second time, the lieutenant had interrupted him. Angriff paused and narrowed his eyes. The lieutenant looked down and Angriff decided to let it go.

"Major Kordibowski is an intelligence specialist on my staff. I value both of these men's opinions,

Lieutenant, and they both think you're the man for the job of heading up this new task force. Any comments or questions, gentlemen?"

"Just one," Fleming said. "How did you pick your code name, Lieutenant? Green Ghost, right?"

"That's right, General Fleming. It's kind of a long story. It goes back to when I was a kid... the night my mother died. It was part of a dream, I think. I'm not sure I'm supposed to tell you more." Angriff noticed when the young man cut a quick glance in his direction, and got the feeling he was missing something.

Fleming held up a large hand with manicured nails and cuticles, but calluses on his fingertips and palms. "Quite right, Lieutenant, you're not. Nor is it important. I was simply curious. I've got nothing more, General Angriff."

"Major?"

"Nothing that we have not already discussed, sir."

"I told you before I couldn't answer for him, Rip. Go ahead and ask him."

"Very well. Lieutenant, what would motivate you to die for your country, knowing that you might be publicly disavowed for the actions that got you killed?"

"I don't see it as a big deal either way, Major. If I'm dead, I won't care what they say about me."

"What if you are taken prisoner?"

"I won't be."

"But if you are?"

"I won't be."

"You cannot say that for certain. You could be knocked unconscious, bound, and unable to harm yourself before the enemy could torture information from you. What I would like to know is, if you are in charge of a clandestine task force, a... a..."

"I told you to call it what it is, Rip," Angriff said. "It's a black ops team."

"Have it your way, sir. Lieutenant, you will be privy to a great deal of information that certain of our enemies would do anything to possess, so I'm trying to discover your motivation for volunteering for this assignment."

"I..." He started to answer, but then stopped.

"Go on, Lieutenant. Now's the time for honesty. Say whatever you need, in whatever way you need to say it."

"All right, General. Major Kor... Kor—"

"Kor-di-bow-sky."

"Thank you. Major Kordibowski. First off, I didn't volunteer for this assignment. I haven't even said I'd take it yet."

"That's true, Rip," Angriff said. "I haven't put the hard sell on, and I'm not going to. Not on this one. I hope he takes it, I think he's the right man, but it's up to him and so far I don't have an answer."

"Second," the lieutenant said, almost as if Angriff hadn't spoken, "I'd chew glass before I let myself get taken."

"Chew glass?" Angriff asked.

"Kill myself, sir. Cyanide used to be issued in glass ampoules, so biting on one meant you were chewing the glass."

"What d'ya know, I learned something. I knew about the ampoules and cyanide and all, but I never heard the expression *chewing glass* before. Now I know. But Lieutenant, the major makes a good point. What *is* your motivation for accepting this assignment? Assuming you say yes."

23

The young officer's blue eyes looked directly into Angriff's, and the general felt a strange affinity for the man. They'd never met before, he'd asked, but still it was there. Some instinct had told him this was the man for the job and that the lieutenant would never let him down. He'd told Fleming about it and his best friend had merely laughed.

"It's hard to explain, General."

"Try."

After a deep breath, the lieutenant answered. "I never met my father until recently. I'd been told he was dead, but that wasn't right. It turns out he's a great man and I want to follow in his steps. He has served the country his entire life, and I want to do the same."

"I'm sure he's very proud of you."

"He isn't yet, sir. But I hope that someday he is."

"I don't know anything about him, Lieutenant, but if he was here right now I'll bet he'd tell you to take the job."

"You really think so, General?"

"I do. If you were my son, that's what I'd tell you to do."

"All right then, General. I'm your man."

#

CHAPTER 3

"No good decision was ever made in a swivel chair."
Lieutenant General George S. Patton

Camp Zippo, Djibouti
1544 hours, July 14, 2012

After Fleming and Kordibowski left, Angriff asked the lieutenant to stay for a moment. "You've got a big job in front of you," he said, launching into the speech he'd rehearsed a dozen times. "Everything the task force does must be different from standard U.S. military protocols. No more saluting superior officers or returning salutes if they are given. If you get any blowback from that, try to handle it yourself. Only as a last resort are you to have them contact USAC, and by last resort I mean to spring you from prison or avoid getting hanged. Don't use my name, ever. Everything you do from this moment forward must be divorced from the U.S. military. If within your mission parameters you find yourself blocked by anybody in our armed forces, you'll have a number to call to let us know and we'll take it from there. *That* we can straighten out fast.

"If you absolutely have to give a cover, you're independent contractors—"

"Mercs?"

"Mercs. You are never to use each other's rank

or service branch, or share any personal details. From now on it's code names only. Radio procedures must be changed from standard regulations. Even your uniforms have to be non-American.

"You can use any American weapons that are easily available on the market, or from an ally, such as the M16 or M4, but not something unique to us. You can also use gear from any other country in the world. The more foreign gear you use, the better. Any questions?"

"A couple, sir."

"No more sirs."

"Right... okay, what do I call you?"

"You can call me general, just forget the officer courtesies."

"Do you have a code name, General?"

"Me? No. Why should I?"

"You're the creator of this task force. You should have a name. What about Saint Nick?"

Angriff couldn't stifle the bark of a laugh. "Me, Santa Claus? That image would certainly amuse a number of people. Sure, why not?"

"For the record then, what's this task force called?"

"You tell me."

The younger man didn't have to think for long. "As I see it, we're all gonna be dead to the world at large, except we're not really dead. We're still walking around, like zombies. No name, no identity, just each other and the mission. Task Force Zombie."

"It's not what I would have picked, but if you like it, then Zombie it is."

"Can we design our own patch, Saint?"

Angriff smiled at the distant memory of a young woman he'd known during his days at West Point,

the one who'd vanished without warning, leaving on-
ly a goodbye note so he wouldn't worry about her.
She would find the name Saint very inaccurate.
"That doesn't seem like a good idea."

"Mercenaries have names. There's nothing weird
about having a logo or patch. We just won't use it
for anything having to do with the U.S. military. It's
good for morale."

"Tell you what, I'll think about it."

"Thank you, s–" Green Ghost stopped, and then
started again. "Thank you, Saint."

#

Chapter 4

"The truth of the matter is that you always know the right thing to do. The hard part is doing it."
General Norman Schwarzkopf

0917 hours, July 18, 2012
Meck Island, Kwajalein Atoll

Sweat dripped from Green Ghost's nose and soaked his black T-shirt. He ignored the heat shimmering upward from the concrete of the heli-pad as he stalked toward the small building at the foot of the boat ramp. Dust and sand swirled at his back as the Sikorsky SH-60 Seahawk took off.

The building itself was a small storage hangar, with an even smaller office facing the waters of the lagoon to the west. He glanced into the hangar but didn't see anyone, and walked around looking for signs of other people. Through a window into the office he saw heads. Opening first the office screen door and then the heavier inside door, he felt a blast of chilled air wash over him as he entered.

Fourteen people packed the little room. They'd come by boat earlier in the morning but weather over the Pacific had delayed him getting to Kwajalein Island, which in turn caused him to miss the boat with the rest of his team. When he stepped into the room, all the faces turned his way, but instead of closing the door behind him, he motioned them to follow him outside. Several of them swore, one louder than the rest, and Green Ghost heard it even ten feet beyond the door.

"Another fuckin' princess."

He wanted to squint but didn't, remembering Angriff's advice about his *tell*. Instead he didn't react at all, didn't even turn around, but marched around the corner and into the hangar without looking back. Although sheltered from the sun, the metal roof caused convection inside a space large enough for one good-sized helicopter and no more. The interior was dark, made even more so by walking through the blinding sunlight to get there. Green Ghost had worn his sunglasses, so removing those made it better for him.

He stood with folded arms until they'd all assembled against the far wall. "You people seemed a little crowded in that air-conditioned office, and if there's one thing a princess like me doesn't like, it's being crowded. So I hope this nice, hot hangar is more to your liking."

Their faces began to coalesce from ill-defined shadow to something more distinct.

"My name is Green Ghost. For those of you who don't know, or weren't listening when it was explained to you, this is a new unit, with new mission parameters and new security measures. Your interaction with the outside world as you knew it is over. Henceforth you are anonymous, men and women without a country. If this is not acceptable to you, if you don't think you're a good fit for this unit, now's your last chance to say so. If you bug out now, nothing happens; you go back to your regular rank and career. If, however, you stay, then your life will never be the same."

He paused long enough for his audience to process the words. "We're gonna introduce ourselves first, and that should give everybody time to think about their decision."

"Is this first grade?" somebody stage-whispered. It was the same voice that had made the princess remark.

"Let's start with the comedian, and remember, code names only."

Several in the front rank turned to a shorter figure behind them. Green Ghost couldn't make out any details in the dim lighting.

"The name's Vapor, because—"

Green Ghost cut him off. Although it was the last voice he'd ever thought to hear on a desolate island in the middle of the Pacific Ocean, he recognized it. "Because you fart a lot."

Everybody laughed, except Vapor. When they quieted down, Vapor spoke over them. "Because I move as quiet as a mist."

Green Ghost kept his arms crossed, but let a smile enter his voice. "Bullshit. I think it's the fart thing."

The others rattled off their colorful names. Wingnut; Claw; a scowling linebacker-type named Adder; Awahili, which was Cherokee for *eagle* and got shortened to simply Hili; Judge; Gomorrah; a stocky woman named Esther; D.J. Pain, *"drop the D.J."* he was told immediately, and became simply Pain; a second woman named Frosty; One-Eye, *"you must be a dick"*; Zeus; Nimcha; and the third female, Donner, because *"every team needs a reindeer."*

When they'd finished, Green Ghost walked up and down the line, staring into their eyes. None turned away.

"Questions?"

"I got one," said a man who matched Green Ghost's six feet, but was more heavily muscled.

Green Ghost pointed at him. "Is it Claw?" The man nodded. "Ask away."

"What are the odds we walk away from this in one piece?"

"I don't know. Probably bad, if you mean retire from this duty and go live a normal life. But if you're still dreaming of that, you're in the wrong place. You need to cut your losses and rejoin your regular unit."

Claw rubbed his chin. "I think I'll stay."

"Good answer. Look, I'm not the kind of guy to blow smoke up your ass; we're gonna get the shittiest jobs the American military and government security agencies can think to give us. I have no doubt of it. They'll fuck us over in a heartbeat if it means covering their own asses; you can bet the farm on that. But so what? The fact is we get to go places and do things other people can only read about in novels, or watch on the History Channel. If that doesn't get your nipples hard, you're in the wrong place. But if it does, then you've found your family. Any more questions?"

"What's the chain of command?" It was the biggest man among them, the one named Adder. Green Ghost hated pre-judging people, but he'd disliked the man from the first instant he'd seen him. His service record, while indicating that Adder always felt like he should be in charge, was also impeccable and even impressive.

"We're gonna go over all that soon, but for the moment all you need to know is that I'm in charge. Now, if there's no more questions for me, then I've got one for y'all... is anybody a no-go?" Nobody spoke. "Last chance; speak now or forever hold your peace." Still nothing. "In that case, y'all are all now part of Task Force Zombie. You officially no longer exist. Anybody not know why we got that name?"

"Because we're all dead men walking?" It was the man named Vapor, the same guy who'd spoken up earlier and the man whose voice Green Ghost had recognized.

"That, yeah, but mostly because anybody stupid enough to join this unit needs brains." Some of them chuckled; the rest scowled. Vapor was too far in shadow for Green Ghost to see which he'd done. "But what the fuck, right? The world never liked us anyway."

Cases of water were stacked in the corner, and Green Ghost dismissed them to grab a drink and get to know each other before they got started on the first team-building exercise. He shook hands with several of them he'd run across in his previous missions with the Rangers, but excused himself to find the wiseguy named Vapor. He knew the voice and face as well as he did his own, but how the man had become a Zombie was impossible to understand.

The face belonged to his best friend, Aaron.

"Well, fuck me," he said.

The smaller man clapped him on the arm. "I don't roll that way, man. You're too muscled up now. You look like one of the Village People. Your sister, on the other hand..."

"She'd bite your throat out."

"Like I don't know it. But she *is* hot, in a psychotic kind of way. Are we supposed to be talking about family?"

"No, but we're not supposed to know each other, either."

"I"ll be glad to forget you."

"Fuck you." Green Ghost dropped his voice. "So what are you doing here? You didn't even play sports in high school, so what are you doing in the fucking special forces? Much less Zombie."

"Nobody was more surprised than me, N—" He caught himself. "—Green Ghost. By the way, nice name. I remember when you got it, about the dream and all. I joined the Army not long after you did. About halfway through basic, I started getting good at shit like marksmanship and rappelling and all that bullshit they put you through. I was more shocked than even my drill sergeant, who thought I'd be the platoon fuckup."

"You're already ours."

"I love you, too. Anyway, people with shiny stuff on their uniforms kept sending me to schools and stuff, and the next thing I knew I was in the 75th Regiment and being recruited by Special Forces."

"As a meat eater?"

"Fuckin'-A. Then I heard about this and now it's high school reunion time."

"You can't tell anybody we're friends."

"Moi? Would I do that?"

"I mean it. You do that and you're washed, friend or no friend."

For one of the few times in his life, Green Ghost saw his best friend's face grow solemn. "I won't say a word, boss. I really want this gig... bad. I've gotta weird feeling it's gonna lead to some epic places. Whatever happens, it beats Little Hell."

#

CHAPTER 5

*"The soldier is the army. No army is better than its
soldiers."*
Lieutenant General George S. Patton

0751 hours local time, September 14, 2012
Shemya Island, Alaska

Painted gray by the Marines, the Gulfstream C-
20G had lifted off from Kaneohe five hours earlier
and cruised at 32,000 feet northwest over the Pacific
Ocean. By that point, the aircraft was closer to Sibe-
ria's Kamchatka Peninsula than mainland Alaska,
and its destination was nothing more than a speck
on a map. Without the latest avionics, finding tiny
Shemya Island would have been nearly impossible
over such a long distance, especially with the low
clouds hanging over the North Pacific and extending
into the Bering Sea.

The plane had sixteen seats, one more than they
needed, although it could have held up to 26 passengers. This arrangement gave them all more leg
room and all of them used the time to catch up on
lost sleep, all except Green Ghost. Somehow he
tuned out the siren's call of the steady engine pulse
and kept his eyes open, studying his team and
thinking of who over the past two months had
emerged as people he could trust, and who hadn't.

Despite drooping lids, he fought to stay awake and think.

He lost. A hand shook him awake and he looked into the face of the navigator.

"Half an hour to touchdown."

"Right."

"Can I ask you something?"

Green Ghost's expression went blank, as he'd trained himself to do instead of squinting. He didn't answer, hoping the guy would get the message. But apparently, since he wasn't wearing any insignia, the Marine lieutenant wasn't intimidated.

"Who are you guys? Somebody said you're mercs... I heard that's jacked up with cash."

"Didn't you get orders about asking questions?"

"I'm sorry, you're right. I shouldn't have asked that."

"No, you shouldn't. Obey your orders next time."

The officer paused and Green Ghost saw the debate taking place in his mind, reflected on his twitching face and in the V-shaped lines on his forehead. The man didn't know why Ghost's people were considered VIPs, and now he was debating if they *were* VIPs. "I just wondered what your name was, but like I said, I'm sorry if I was out of line."

"We don't have names, Lieutenant, because we don't exist." This time he made a point of turning his neck to see the lieutenant's name badge. "Right, Lieutenant Ballard?"

"Yeah... right. We didn't fly you to nowhere Alaska because you aren't really here, but even if you were, you're nameless, so I couldn't tell anybody who you were. Even though you don't exist."

"Now you've got it."

The Marine walked down the aisle back to the

cockpit, avoiding crossed legs sticking out from the seats. "Nameless," Green Ghost said, trying out how it sounded. "The Nameless... yeah, that's it."

Once the cockpit door was secured behind the lieutenant, Green Ghost got out of his seat. With a sudden burst of energy, he woke up the others and waited for them to pee or get a bottle of water before addressing them.

"I thought of our code name."

"I thought Zombie was our code name," said the pain-in-his-butt that was Adder. The man never missed a chance to question Green Ghost's authority.

"Zombie is the code name for the task force." His tone let Adder know there were things he knew, that Adder didn't, because Adder wasn't in command. "But that's a code name within the military frame-work. We need something that doesn't directly tie us to the U.S. armed forces in any way, for use in situations where we might be overheard."

"So let's hear it." Adder made it sound like a command. Green Ghost's stony face served as a warning, one which his team had seen and grown to understand over the last two months.

"We're the Nameless."

Winds at ground level were out of the southwest, so the Gulfstream circled around the tiny dot of land below. Out the portside window, most of what they saw was a mosaic of gray. Low clouds of light and medium gray occasionally broke, giving a glimpse of a darker gray landmass, in a charcoal gray ocean ripped by whitecaps.

"I liked that other island better," Vapor said.

"That's the bleakest place I've ever seen," said a

new voice. They were all surprised that it had been Gomorrah's. One of the youngest Zombies, he'd barely said a dozen words in the past week.

Green Ghost held onto the overhead compartment as he leaned over and inspected Shemya Island with them. It was perfect.

"All right, listen up. That is Aereckson Air Station down below. It is no longer an air force base; it's a refueling station and emergency landing strip. *But...* there are Air Force personnel still on the island, which means there will be a junior officer on hand. And if he's stationed at such a shithole in the middle of the Bering Sea, you can bet he's the biggest fuckup in the Air Force, and he's gonna have an attitude."

"How come it can't be a woman?" Esther asked with raised eyebrows.

"There's no woman in the world bitchy enough to get sent down there."

"You haven't met my ex-wife." Green Ghost couldn't tell who'd said that. It sounded like Frosty, but her voice was deeper than Vapor's, so he couldn't be sure.

"Whoever's down there, they're gonna want to know who we are, our outfit, all that shit. Remember, you do *not* salute and you don't return one. As far as they're concerned, you're anonymous mercs, period. If somebody demands your name, tell 'em to fuck off. If they give you any more shit, get me involved."

"It's about to get good." It was Adder who spoke that time.

"None of that shit! If any of you *start* trouble, you're gone. Is that understood? This ain't playtime; the people paying for this circus want us operational

a-sap. Once we touch down, grab your gear and follow me."

The pilot goosed the engine in a forlorn attempt
to overcome the turbulence. Even as the noise level
increased, the Zombies all talked over each other.

"As long as we don't have to shoot SCAR-17s,
I'm good with anything."

"Sounds like a personal problem."

"Aside from the damned things jamming all the
time, I hate that fuckin' reciprocating bolt."

"Amen, brudda," said One-Eye. "I was outside
the wire of a COP" — *combat outpost* — "talkin' to a
village chief when we got hit with incoming AK fire. I
grabbed my SCAR by the magazine and returned
fire, and that fuckin' bolt almost took my thumb
off."

"That's its official name, right, the *fuckin'* reciprocating bolt?"

"The fucker's too damned big, that's its problem."

"I *do* like that it can shoot a .308 round if you
need the distance."

"I hated that scope. It was like lookin' through a
toilet paper roll. I had to clear a house with one. I'm
just lucky it was empty."

Green Ghost scowled and did something he'd
never done before. He shouted. "Shut the fuck up!"

That quieted them, all except Adder. As usual,
he had to get in one more comment. Both he and
Green Ghost knew it was the big man's way of showing that he, Adder, should have been in charge.
"SCAR's way too loud. If you're trying to engage,
communicate, and stay alive, you don't want to be
standing next to the guy shooting one of those."

"I said shut up, Adder!" snapped Green Ghost.

This time he pointed at the offender.

The biggest of all the Zombies, Adder showed by his reaction that he wasn't used to being singled out for public rebuke. Wide eyes and open mouth betrayed his shock at being called out like that, but that quickly faded into a squinting scowl. At that moment, Green Ghost could see something in his eyes change, and instinctively knew there would someday be a showdown between them.

"We just wanted to make sure you heard us," said Vapor, trying to relieve the tension. Green Ghost's glare made him look down.

The Sikorsky helicopter skimmed the breakers at 100 feet, close enough so that its fifteen passengers could smell the brine of the seas below. The bitter temperature drooped lower as wind swirled through the passenger compartment, reddening and deadening their noses and the tips of their ears.

"I liked that last island better," Vapor said.

Green Ghost turned his way, determined not to show how badly the cold hurt his lungs. "You've already said that."

"No, I meant that island we just left. I liked that better than wherever we're going to now. It had satellite TV."

"How do you know we're not heading for Jamaica?"

"Are we?"

"Not even close."

Fifteen minutes later they crossed the rocky beach of an island even smaller than Shemya. Hard surf broke over a line of boulders just inland from the Bering Sea, with soil so devoid of life it appeared to be an alien landscape. Only in spots did vagrant grass sprout through volcanic rocks. Leaning out first the port side and then the starboard, they could all see the island's width of some five hundred yards. Length measured just over 700 yards.

"This dump got a name?" somebody asked.

"Whatever Alaskan is for *asshole of the universe.*"

A third voice chimed in. "Alaskan ain't a language, dumbass. The Eskimos speak Aleut."

From there it devolved into raucous argument and Green Ghost had to smile. He thought about telling them it was named Nizki Island, but didn't. They were beginning to sound like a cohesive unit and he didn't want to interrupt the good-natured squabbling.

Buffeting winds made the approach dangerous. The island had constant winds of anywhere between 10 and 40 miles per hour. After circling three times to find a direction which would allow a safe approach, all three helicopters landed in a spray of gravel and rock. After unloading their cargo of tents, food, water, communications gear, weapons, and ammo, they took off again, leaving the Zombies all alone.

Aside from a few grumbles, however, none of them said anything. Instead, without a word, all fifteen people broke down the gear. Some erected tents while others built a fire pit or stacked food and water containers. Within half an hour, the camp was ready for the onrushing night.

They spent the rest of the day breaking down the Chinese field radios they'd been issued, learning how to repair them, clean them, and use them. Then they field-tested the new communications protocols they'd developed back at Kwajalein, using the United States Army Infantry Intercom system they were already familiar with. Approval was given to use it because not only was it the best in the world, but it was also readily available on the black market.

Once night fell, it was time to get used to the Russian night vision gear they'd have to use in place of their own It wasn't as good as the latest American models, but during the training exercise, it would have to do.

#

CHAPTER 6

"Some people are just assholes and there's nothing you can do about it."
Vapor

1414 hours, September 17, 2012
Nizki Island, Alaskan Aleutians

Winds buffeted Green Ghost as he rappelled down the cliff face high over the breakers below. The team building exercise relied on each member to help the next. No one line was long enough to reach the bottom, so instead four members each had one quarter of what was needed. They would drive spikes for the next member to descend, and so on. There was no safety net. If a spike wasn't driven properly and the Zombie fell, there was nothing to stop them being seriously injured, or dying.

Ghost was the third of the four, and was near enough to the sea to feel salt spray coating his legs, when the infantry intercom attached to his helmet chirped up.

It was Wingnut. "Green Ghost, trouble at base camp. Over."

Fuck! "What's the story?"

"Some Air Force asshole demands to know what we're doing here and who we are."

"Did you tell him to fuck off?"

"Yeah, that got guns trained on me."

"Shit. All right, I'll be there a-sap. "

It took half an hour to coordinate the climb back to the top, and another fifteen minutes to return to base using the one Humvee they'd taken to the cliff. Beside the main tent, Wingnut stood with an AKM aimed at two beefy guards flanking a red-faced major in Air Force fatigues.

"Are you in charge of this circus?" the major said.

"Who's asking?"

The major's face deepened into maroon. "I'm Major William K. Karns of the United States Air Force. This is Air Force property under my command, and while I don't know who the hell you think you are, you either tell me what I want to know or I'll have you arrested before the sun goes down!"

"No, you won't."

"Sergeant, arrest this man!"

The sergeant, a stocky man with the weather-worn face of a career soldier, stood behind the major. At the order, he rolled his eyes but drew his sidearm.

Wingnut raised the rifle to his shoulder, the barrel never leaving the major's florid face. The other three Air Force Security Officers raised their rifles.

"Stand your men down, Major, before somebody gets shot and you're either dead, or your career is over," Green Ghost said.

"Sergeant," Karns said, nearly shouting over a strong gust off the beach, "you are authorized to use whatever force is necessary to arrest these men!"

"Before you do anything that stupid, I suggest you contact Special Operations Command and ask them about what we're doing here."

Karns had the slack-faced features and wrinkles around the eyes that gave the impression of being a dullard, and usually Green Ghost didn't judge people by their looks. In the gray world of special operations, that was dangerous. But in Karns' case, he was tempted to make an exception. The man was a cartoon. He'd heard about officers like this, but in his experience even the bad ones were well intentioned. Not this guy. No wonder he was stationed in the middle of nowhere.

"I'll do that once you're in custody. Now, for the last time, Sergeant Berecz, arrest these men!"

Green Ghost stopped them by holding up his hand, palm out. He reached for the SAT-phone on his belt, which instantly brought all four rifles to bear on him. The four tense Air Force Security men watched every move as he showed them the phone, turned it out so they could see it wasn't a weapon, and punched in a number.

"Put that down!" Karns said. Green Ghost ignored him.

Someone answered on the first ring. "Code?"

"G.G. Alpha."

"Vector?"

"Saint Nick."

Seven seconds later the voice of Nick Angriff came on the line. "Go."

Major Karns picked that moment to yell at him again to put the phone down and his hands up.

Angriff heard it. "Who is that?"

"Major William K. Karns."

"Gyrene?"

"Bird boy."

"Got it."

Click.

"Okay, Major, you win." Green Ghost motioned for Wingnut to drop his rifle.

Karn's eyes widened with triumph as his loose skin twisted into what Ghost realized was a smile. The sergeant and his men were quick to pat them down and handcuff them. They tried leaving the Zombies' hands in front, but Karns ordered them to pull them tight behind their backs.

Once they were secured, Karns leaned in close to Green Ghost's face. His breath smelled like fish. "I don't know who you are, or who you think you are, but nobody messes with me. Now, tell me everything."

"Now?"

As if to underscore his point, an icy breeze sent gravel skittering across the ground.

"Right now."

Behind the major's shoulder, he saw the sergeant accept a radio handset from one of the other men.

"I don't think we have time."

"No? Why is that?"

Green Ghost pointed with his head. Karns turned to see the sergeant approaching with the phone-like handset extended before him.

"Major, it's AFSOC. They say it's urgent."

Karns squinted just the slightest bit, but that tiny change told Green Ghost everything he needed to know. The major had realized something was going very wrong. The whole point about postings to places such as the outer islands of Alaska was so that higher headquarters like Air Force Special Operations Command never had to deal with them. Snatching the handset, he walked into a patch of grayish reeds near the beach.

"He seems like a sweetheart," Green Ghost said to the sergeant. There was no response, nor had he expected one. For all the sergeant knew, he was *Spetsnaz*. Green Ghost had a clear view of Karns' back, so when the major turned to look out to sea, wheeled, and stalked back toward them, he turned and held out his hands. "Get the key ready."

"Release them," Karns snapped, as if the whole mess was the sergeant's fault. "Now!" Then, taking a deep breath, he donned as fake of a smile as he could manage. "On behalf of the United States Air Force Special Operations Command, please accept my apologies for the misunderstanding. If I can help you in any way moving forward, my command is at your disposal."

"Thank you, Major."

Karns opened his mouth to say something else, thought better of it, and left.

The sergeant waited for him to get out of earshot before turning toward Green Ghost. "You're lucky, man... we gotta live with that dickhead."

Scud clouds blew low over their heads as the Zombies huddled in a circle and ate MREs. The training parameters didn't allow for any lights or electrically powered devices, so the flavors were un-known until they opened the package. Judge lost the MRE lottery because he got the veggie omelet, also known as the *Vomelet*. It was almost universally considered vile, except for one person, who loved them: Wingnut. In his turn, Wingnut got the meat-balls with marinara, which he hated but Judge loved. Others grumbled about their selections, but Green Ghost shut them all up.

"It could have been worse. They could have all been rat-fucked, so count your blessings, you heroes."

"Then they would all have been vomelets," said Vapor.

Wingnut gave a thumb's up.

"Or chicken fajitas."

"Those are flat-out gross."

One by one, they pulled the sleeping bags tight and moved closer to share their warmth. The low temperature that night would only hit the high 20s, not cold enough to freeze extremities but more than cold enough to suck.

"Tell me again why we can't use the tents," said Pain. The shiver in his voice was faint, but audible.

"Consider it a team-building exercise."

Frosty had to shout to be heard over the roar of surf against the rocky shore. "Anybody grabs my ass and they'll get back a stump."

In the near-absolute darkness, Green Ghost could only hear the laugh in Esther's voice. "Well, never mind then."

"You're an exception. I was talkin' to Wingnut."

The banter died down as the wet air seeped through into the sleeping bags. Wind velocity picked up until only a near-shout could be heard, even from the men, and that required too much energy. Eventually there was nothing left except closely huddled cocoons.

0231 hours, September 18, 2012

The buzzing of the satellite phone caused Green Ghost to squint at the blurry blue numbers on the face of his watch. Like a neon sign on a foggy night, they slowly came into focus: 0231 hours, local time.

"Green Ghost," he said, licking his dry lips to moisten them.

"Top rank," replied a metallic voice, which told him it was a scrambled message from General Angriff. "Ticks at thirty, all in. Go."

Top priority from General Angriff, pickup in thirty minutes, bring the whole team.

Adrenaline fully woke him within seconds. "Uppfattat." Swedish for *roger that.* As an added security measure, common radio chatter would sometimes be in languages other than English. Jumping up, he moved among the sleeping bags and nudged his team awake. "We're on deck and outta here in thirty minutes."

Groans in the dark were loud enough to hear even over the crashing waves less than fifty yards distant.

"Where to now?" Green Ghost thought it was Adder who asked.

"No idea. But this is top rank."

"Whoa." This time he recognized Vapor's voice, echoed by several others. "No shit? Saint Nick himself?"

"No shit. My guess is something's grade-A fucked and we're on deck to fix it."

\#

CHAPTER 7

"I'm fed up to the ears with old men dreaming up wars for young men to die in."
Former B-24 pilot and Senator George S. McGovern, whose plane, the Dakota Queen, once had 110 holes in it from flak over Germany

0343 hours local time, September 21, 2012
Diego Garcia Island

The C-130 had slowed nearly to stall speed when it touched down at Naval Support Facility Diego Garcia, bounced once, and skidded down the runway in a squeal of braking tires. The fifteen Zombies barely noticed, as most were still sound asleep. After helicoptering back to Aereckson Air Station on Shemya Island, the same Gulfstream that had flown them north flew them south again to Joint Base Pearl Harbor-Hickam on Oahu, where they changed planes to an Airbus A-330 MRTT. Instead of standard US Air Force light gray paint, the giant aircraft had been painted an overall dark gray-green, with no marks or serial numbers. Warnings at various places around the plane's exterior were in a language Green Ghost knew was Czech, even though he couldn't read them.

The plane's interior had been fitted out to carry up to eighty people in oversized chairs that reclined flat and were arranged so they could all be used as beds. Beyond that was a huge cargo space, now mostly empty. A large storage locker in front of the cargo area was filled with foil-covered meals, while a refrigerator contained sodas and water.

"No fuckin' beer," Esther had said.

Before takeoff, Green Ghost had asked the flight engineer who owned the aircraft and what it was used for, but got no answer. Then he'd gone to sleep. That had been twenty-one hours ago. He'd gotten up three times to pee but was sound asleep again when the same flight engineer shook him awake. Much to Green Ghost's surprise, the man spoke.

"We have to refuel," he said in a heavy German or Austrian accent. "Get your people up. I am told you will have a visitor." Since in German the *w* sound is a combination *f* and *v*, the words *we* and *will* came out as *vee* and *vill*.

There were only two bathrooms on board. Ten minutes later, four Zombies were still in line when the portside door opened and a man came through, wearing an American combat uniform in the universal camouflage pattern, with three black stars on a patch worn just below the sternum. A patrol cap with three stars across the front was low on the man's forehead, above close-cropped hair so blonde it was hard to say if it was pale yellow or white. When they saw his ice blue eyes, everyone recognized their famous commanding officer, Lieutenant General Nicholas T. Angriff.

Vapor started to call 'ten–hut' but caught himself after getting out "Ten—" Angriff shot him a glance but said nothing about the slip. Despite keeping quiet and not saluting, the entire group nevertheless stiffened. If it wasn't coming to full attention, it was close.

"Saint Nick," Green Ghost said, not sure if he should shake Angriff's hand or let it go. He decided to let it go. "I'm surprised to see you here."

"Relax, smoke 'em if you've got 'em." Nobody lit up, even the ones who wanted to. "How's the training going?"

"As well as can be expected. We're knocking out procedures, call signs, organization, all that good stuff. But it's hard to unlearn stuff that was hammered into you."

"But you're getting there?"

"Yes."

"Good, I'm glad to hear it." He came closer, put a friendly hand on Green Ghost's shoulder, and steered him away from the others. When he spoke again, it was in a low voice. "Have you picked your leaders yet?"

"I've got a pretty good idea of who I want."

"Organization?"

"Fifteen's an odd number, but I think eventually I'd like squads of twelve with four three-person sections. That gives a lot of flexibility. Each section will be cross-trained for planning, administrative, reserve, and assault roles."

"What if you had to go right now?"

"Do we?"

"Humor me."

"Well, I'd organize five three-man sections, three assault, one in reserve, and one in support for heavy weapons and communications."

"Good, I like it. Sounds like you've got a handle on things."

"Like I said, we're getting there."

"Call your people together, Lieu—" Angriff stopped and smiled. "Now I'm doing it. I need to speak with everybody, Green Ghost." When they were all gathered around, he sat next to Esther and leaned forward, hands on knees. The skin of his face had always had the lean, weather-worn look of a combat soldier, but now Green Ghost thought the lines around his jowls and eyes seemed deeper. "There's not much time so I'll get right to the point. As of this moment, Task Force Zombie is operational. You've got your first mission, if you'll take it."

The Zombies all looked at each other. "We have a choice?" Green Ghost said.

"Before we get into that, if anybody feels they can't undertake a mission that might result in not only your death, but also your disgrace in the eyes of the world and your own country, now's the time to say so. Nobody will hold it against you if you bow out on this one, but if that's your choice, then you need to step off the plane now. Get your gear and go."

Nobody spoke for a full five seconds, which seemed like forever. "I signed off for the fun stuff, so let's get going." To nobody's surprise, Adder had been the speaker.

Angriff twitched a half-grin. "Anybody out?" he said.

Green Ghost met the eyes of every one of the Zombies, nodded at them, and waited for a return nod. Once they'd all done that, he turned back to Angriff. "We're all in, Saint. So... why the choice?"

"As far as you know, the president hasn't approved this one, or the SecDef or Homeland or anybody in the chain of command at or above General Steeple, Chairman of the Joint Chiefs. I can't tell you who authorized it; that's above your clearances. All I *can* tell you is that if this one goes sideways, the way it'll play out is that you all left the military and that was the last the United States knew about you."

That brought deafening silence and the stares that subordinates give their superior officers when hearing about a terrible battle plan. They'd known all that all along, but now they faced the reality of it. Angriff took time to meet the eyes of all fifteen of them as Green Ghost watched. He thought his team's reactions ranged from *Is it too late to back out?* to *When do we start?* When Angriff came to him, he tried not to show any reaction, but his left eye twitched as it did when he was under pressure, a reaction he'd worked hard to suppress. It was a holdover from the old *tell* of narrowing his eyes. Obviously there was more work to do there.

"Make no mistake, since TFZ was my idea, it's all our asses on the line with this one. I'm betting on you, each and every one of you. And just so you know, yeah, it's worth it to me to take that risk. We need you if we're going to win this war. Now, let's get down to it. What have you heard about the attack on our embassy in Benghazi?"

"Nothing," Green Ghost said, answering for them all. "We've been on a rock in the Bering Sea. What attack?"

The general shook his head and took a cigar out of his breast pocket. "Anybody else want one?"

They all shook their heads *no*, except for Adder. "Sure thing," he said. Angriff handed one over along with a small box of wooden matches. He watched as the big man stuck the cigar in his mouth and lit it like someone would light a cigarette, pulling hard to get the ash glowing. Then he took back the matches and carefully toasted the foot of his own cigar before lighting it.

"Nine days ago in Benghazi, at approximately zero-nine-forty local time, a Muslim terrorist group

53

called Ansar al-Sharia attacked the American embassy in that city. Hundreds of men armed with hand grenades and automatic weapons entered the embassy compound and killed our ambassador to Libya and a Foreign Service agent. Six hours later, a mortar attack on a CIA building killed two contractors."

He paused to draw on the cigar. "Now before you ask, we don't know if this group is affiliated with al-Qaeda or not, although a few hours prior al-Zawahiri had called for attacks in Libya. The president says there's no correlation, that the attacks were motivated by a movie they found offensive." Again he stopped, and Green Ghost could tell he was gauging their reactions. "But whether he believes that or it's just a smokescreen to hide future actions, regardless of the reason... that's all just background for why I'm here. Libya won't involve you... we can use regular special forces there if we need to. What we need you for involves Egypt."

Vapor began to speak but Angriff held up his hand. "Let me finish first; we don't have much time. This is a closed loop op. Besides you, me, the chief of intelligence for this mission, Major Kordibowski, and a few other select personnel, including the higher-ups who signed off on it, nobody else knows about this mission. It *must* stay that way. Is that clear? All of our asses are on the line here, so any breach of security will be considered a court-martial offense. If it goes to hell, I'll do whatever I can to shield you, and you plead that you were just following orders, but I can't guarantee that'll work. But this is precisely the kind of operation you all signed up for.

"Three days after the attacks in Benghazi, I was contacted by a high-ranking member of the Egyptian military who's an old acquaintance, and warned that a senior adviser to Ansar al-Sharia had just arrived in Egypt from Libya. That man is your HVT. His name is Alois Steyer, a former Austrian *Jagdkommando* turned mercenary and then arms dealer. You know the type. Arrogant, dangerous, and doesn't give a tinker's damn about anybody but himself. Everything else you need to know about this son of a bitch is on the tablets Major Kordibowski will distribute after I exit the aircraft, but the condensed version is that Steyer doesn't care who gets hurt as long as he gets paid. He seems to have a particular hatred for Americans, although why is as yet unknown.

"As to why he's in Egypt, President Morsi is a member of the Muslim Brotherhood. Nobody knows if he's the die-hard Islamist hardliner some say he is, or if he's a live-and-let-live kind of Islamist."

"Is there such a thing?" Vapor said, then held his hands up in apology.

"I don't know, and for our purposes it doesn't matter. Whatever the reason, we've been given what looks like first class intel on one dangerous son of a bitch who kept those Americans from being rescued. See, we didn't send air support into Benghazi because we knew the enemy had the latest Stingers. I can't tell you where they got them, that's strictly need to know, and honestly I'm not in the loop, either. And I really shouldn't share that with you, but I think you've got a right to know why you're putting your life on the line. I've been told by a reliable source that someone in our own government sold them to Steyer, who then sold them to al-Sharia. Obviously that makes the person in our government a traitor."

"That could be anybody in Washington," Vapor said.

Donner also chirped up. "Do we get to off them, too?"

Green Ghost scowled at all of them. "Knock it off!"

Angriff took two long pulls on his cigar, which flared the ash into orange life, then took it out again. The smile he felt on the inside didn't show on his face. That was exactly the sort of nervous energy needing to be released that he'd hoped to see. "Like I was saying, we couldn't send air support because Ansar al-Sharia had Stingers and we knew it. That was part of their plan, to goad us into helicoptering in reinforcements so they could shoot down the men and the bird, which we would have done had they not had those Stingers. So the person responsible for putting them in Steyer's hands is also responsible for those American deaths."

He paused and walked to the back of the plane, where he knocked the cigar ash from the shortening butt onto the tarmac before returning.

"Steyer is holed up on an island in the Red Sea called Juzur Abū Minqār. A major figure in the Muslim Brotherhood has a compound there; otherwise it's not much of an island, just sand and marsh. It's right off the coast from the city of Hurghada, about a mile long and 2,500 feet wide at its widest point. The highest point is about twenty feet."

Green Ghost raised his hand but Angriff waved it down.

"It's a mile from the city, if that's what you wanted to know. We think his mistress is there with him, a nasty piece of work with the last name Williamson, first name unknown but possibly Holly. The source that reported her there said she's a belly dancer from California and that she's become Steyer's business manager. You'll find her photo in the briefing on the tablets. Your mission is to penetrate the compound, kill Steyer and the girlfriend if she's there, and get out."

He paused to give any of them a chance to protest killing an American citizen, or a female. It was the same ongoing debate they'd all faced on previous missions, namely, if an American sides with terrorists, can they be killed as an enemy combatant, or does that violate the Constitution? Not one Zombie spoke up. In the world of asymmetrical warfare they all inhabited, such niceties were obsolete.

"Good," Angriff said. "As for the woman, she must be a special kind of vicious for hardcore Islamists to deal with a female. There are two islands directly to the east of the compound, both barren. They're called Jazāir Jiftūn, that's the biggest and closest one, and Jiftūn aṣ Ṣaquīr, which is smaller. Distance between them ranges from one to two miles, with shallow water and coral reefs between them. Halo insertion into Jiftūn aṣ Ṣaquīr would be damned near impossible because of its size, and Jazāir Jiftūn is too close to the target. We also believe that Steyer isn't going anywhere for a while, and if we leave him alone for a few days his security will slack off.

"Therefore, this will be a water insertion ten days from today. You'll find full details in your packet, along with the latest satellite images, distances, water depths and currents, etc. Now you can ask questions."

"This is a kill-only mission?" Green Ghost asked.

"I'm not going to sugarcoat this. We want Steyer and the woman dead. There could be other HVTs there, too, and if you get them we won't be sorry, but those two are your targets. This comes from way up."

"And by other HVTs, do you mean Egyptian military personnel?"

"Our source says that if they're on that island, it's because they're Muslim Brotherhood."

"Like their president?" said Vapor, which earned him a stern glance from Green Ghost that Angriff noticed.

"It's all right," Angriff said. "I told them to ask questions. Yes, their president is a member of the Muslim Brotherhood, but I can tell you that most of the Egyptian military recognizes them as a threat to peace and would like to see them outlawed again. The more of them we kill, the fewer there are in the Egyptian military to throw a wrench into any future coup plans. So if they're on that island, they're fair game. But eliminating Steyer is your objective and once that's accomplished you are to exfil immediately."

Adder spoke up next. "Do we plant evidence to pin it on somebody else?"

"That's the beauty of having you people; there's no need for disinformation," Angriff said. The cigar had gone out, but he stuck the butt into the side of his mouth in the pose that everyone knew so well. "You're already somebody else."

#

CHAPTER 8

"Only the dead have seen the end of war."
Plato

0531 hours, September 22, 2012
Diego Garcia Island

One benefit of being in the middle of the Indian Ocean was that the airfield on Diego Garcia could light the runways with as much illumination as necessary. With the blackness of pre-dawn heavy on the surrounding ocean, that meant a lot of light to keep the pilots from losing sight of the horizon. Even taxiing for takeoff, it looked to Angriff as if the C-130 pilot was being extra cautious.

"Looks like they're all going," Major Kordibowski said. He stood beside Angriff, holding an umbrella to ward off the heavy morning mist.

Angriff ignored it, drawing on his second cigar of the day until the ash glowed orange. "I never doubted it for a second," he said. "I knew they'd all go."

"May I ask how you knew, sir?"

"Rip, people like that don't back down from a bad hand, and make no mistake, *this* is a bad hand. They know it as surely as I do."

"Why is that, General?"

"Why is it bad? Huh..." After the grunt, he paused for ten seconds, thinking. Sharing his

59

thoughts with a mere major could come back to bite him on the butt. Yet Kordibowski had been with him a long time now… at last he decided to bring the major into the loop. "Needless to say this is ears only, no repeat. It's bad because if they get caught, they'll be tortured, but that's part of the deal when you live on the sharp edge. They all know that; it's the cost of doing business. What makes this one stink to high heaven is they aren't sure of the purpose of the mission, and I can't tell them because I don't know. This Steyer guy needs to be neutralized, no question about it. But why drop the black flag on him?"

"I am sorry, General, what is the black flag?"

Angriff turned and squinted up at the taller major. "You need to get out more, Rip. Black flag means assassinate, kill him. A guy like Steyer would have priceless intel for the War on Terror, so why not give them the option of capturing him, with a kill being only if you can't bring him in?"

"Oh. I see what you mean."

"Somebody doesn't want him brought in. They want him dead. The questions are who and why."

"Do you have any ideas on that, General?"

"I do, Rip, but I can't share them with you. First, you don't have the clearance, and second… God help me, I don't want to be right."

Aden, Yemen
2025 hours, September 22, 2012

"A lot of people in this city want me dead," said Vapor from the Chevy Suburban's third row.

Green Ghost turned in the car's passenger seat. "Does that include us?"

The convoy of three identical black SUVs sped
down the highway called K6, headed for the Port of
Aden. Behind them, the never-ending line of air-
planes landing and taking off from Aden Interna-
tional Airport made Green Ghost glad they were
safely on the ground. Flying scared the hell out of
him, although he'd never told anybody about his
fear, not even Vapor.

Once they hit the urban area known as
Khormakser, white-clad Yemenis driving European
cars wandered in and out of the traffic, seemingly
oblivious to danger. Their speed varied from crawling along at a near-stop to racing. Aside from the
cars, there were also thousands of scooters darting
in front of, beside, and between cars. And all of it
moved in a choreographed dance that made Green
Ghost wonder if they held city-wide practice ses-
sions.

Nobody bothered trying to see into the SUVs.
Not only were the windows tinted black, but curiosi-
ty in a place like Aden often led to a quick and vio-
lent death. Too many people had too many secrets
they were willing to protect at any cost. Life wasn't
just cheap in Aden; it had no value at all.

The distance to the Port of Aden wasn't that far,
about six miles, but it took half an hour. The sun
had been down for more than two hours and not
every vehicle had headlights. Scooters and motorcy-
cles, in particular, tended to have burned-out bulbs,
so the driver had to keep their speed lower than they
would have preferred. The Zombies had been told
that their drivers could be trusted, but not too far,
which meant *keep mission security tight.*

They stopped portside of an 18,000-ton Norwe-
gian-flagged dry cargo ship named the *Roald*

Amundsen. Dock lights only illuminated the ship's bow and stern, while the loading ramp had internal lights along its sides. Otherwise the *Roald Amundsen* rode heavy and blacked out.

The mission briefing had given only the briefest overview of the ship's history. Launched in the 1950s, it gave the appearance of being lucky to still be afloat. The once black-painted hull was mostly rust-red and the superstructure had several broken railings. It appeared to be missing an anchor, which was incredibly dangerous for an ocean-going vessel. Even the Norwegian flag hanging at the stern had frayed edges. As the fifteen Zombies grabbed their gear and headed up the ramp, Green Ghost prayed it didn't collapse and drop them into the dark waters below.

Once past the first room, a white-bearded man who looked exactly like Green Ghost expected a grizzled Norwegian seaman to look, complete with turtleneck and beard, pointed to a ladder leading down into the bowels of the ship.

"I am Sigurd," he said with a heavy European accent. "Follow me."

Nobody else spoke to them and nobody glanced their way as they descended four decks. Once deep in the hull, they went through a bulkhead into a huge hold that could have been right out of a movie.

Instead of being dark, dank, and wet, like holds on old freighters tended to be, this one was stainless steel that gleamed from overhead halogen lights. The ceiling was low, barely eight feet high. Closed lockers took up the starboard outer bulkhead, and various tables and workstations filled other areas, but none of the Zombies looked at any of that. Instead, they all fixated on the gigantic wall of translucent material taking up most of the port side outer bulkhead, and the six objects within. The Zombies all gaped at seeing something so out of place with the rest of the ship, and turned to Sigurd as though in a choreographed move.

The Norwegian's left cheek twitched in what might have been a smile. "It's exactly what it looks like," he said. "The passage up the Red Sea will take eight days. You will spend that time in here. You have everything you need, and food will be brought to you three times a day. You will find packets over there with your names on them." He pointed to a table near a row of seats in the starboard bulkhead. "Those have your mission parameters and instructions. I suggest you spend your time watching them and getting familiar with your submarines, or you can screw each other for the whole week, I don't care which... but whatever you do, don't leave this hold."

"What if the ship sinks?" Vapor asked.

"Then you drown." Sigurd's brown eyes had a flat, take-no-shit look to them. "Don't let the ship's exterior fool you. It is meant to look old and... what is the English word?"

Vapor responded, "Shitty?"

"Rust bucket?" shouted Gomorrah.

"Dilapidated?" Esther said.

"Thank you," Sigurd said with a nod toward Esther. "That's the word, dilapidated. Old ships don't carry first-class cargoes and therefore don't attract the attention of pirates, or officials looking for bribes. We have made this run twice a month for the last eight months and the Egyptians only stopped us the first time, right before we entered the Suez Canal. But the Sudanese... even with our precautions, they sometimes find reasons to hold ships until certain fees are paid. It would not do for you to be found on board, so don't go wandering around. If we *are* boarded, there might not be time to warn you."

This time it was Green Ghost who spoke up. "Won't they demand to inspect this hold, too?"

"They would, if they knew about it. This hold is in a blister bottom beneath the keel."

"A false bottom?"

"*Nøyaktig slik.*"

"I don't speak Norwegian."

Sigurd grunted. "It means *precisely so.*"

He turned to leave but Green Ghost had one final question.

"Who are you people?"

"I could ask you the same question, but I won't. Just be happy that we're paid to be on your side, whatever side that is. I don't know who you are or why you're on this ship, and I don't want to know."

With that he went back through the watertight door, dogged it, and clanged his way up the ladder and back into the main hull. They could all clearly hear his footfalls.

Inside a semi-circle of steel-reinforced, pressure-proof glass, six identical machines lay secured by heavy steel clamps to twenty-foot metal rails. Behind what was obviously an airlock, in the bulkhead that kept out the sea, a seam marked the meeting place of two large doors. Smaller rails marked the track down which the doors could slide to either side to admit the water. Closed circular vents in the ceiling supplied compressed air to force out the water and clear the lock.

The submarines themselves measured twelve feet long and eight feet wide. Three seats were arranged in a triangular pattern inside a domed glass pod which was flanked by pontoons. High-speed propellers at the rear of each pontoon supplied propulsion. Watertight doors gave access to the bridge seating beneath the domed glass, with a curved control panel allowing access for each rider to the controls located near them. Green Ghost thought they looked like a helicopter and a UFO's love child.

In their mission briefing packets, each Zombie had been given a DVD and self-contained player that looked like a small laptop, along with headphones. A refrigerated locker held bottles of water and a variety of Saudi Arabian soft drinks, tea, and coffee drinks, along with snacks such as yogurt, hummus, and dried fruits. The group split up, with some immediately grabbing a drink and something to munch on while watching the DVD, and others prowling the hold for things like showers, fresh clothes, and the head. A few headed straight for the subs.

"Talk about some sweet tech," Adder said, tracing a finger over the thick windows of one of the submarines. "I wouldn't mind having one of these babies."

"What would you do with it?" said Judge, in a deep drawl with a distinct Texas twang. Lean and tall, the lines in his face made him appear to be the oldest of the Zombies. Green Ghost had watched him closely for the first two weeks of training, anticipating that whatever skills he might once have possessed had eroded over time. After those two weeks, he didn't worry any more.

"Use it to pick up tang, what else?"

From the next submarine over, Esther spoke faster than any of the men. "What species?"

Everybody laughed. It was part of the culture of the teams to give each other shit. But Adder folded his heavily muscled arms and stared at her, and there was no mistaking the anger in his face.

Green Ghost had been standing to one side, observing his command, and moved beside him. "Let it go," he said in a low voice. "She's just messing with you."

Adder's expression didn't change, only now he turned it toward Green Ghost. "You're my C.O. so I gotta do what you tell me, but fuck trying to be my friend."

"What are you so pissed off about, man? I've never done anything to you."

"If you don't know, then you shouldn't be in charge."

"Really?" Green Ghost felt his face getting hot and started to raise his voice, then saw the rest of the team staring at them. He kept his voice low. "If I can't trust you, I can't use you."

"I'll do my job. I'm the best you've got, but we ain't friends. We'll never be friends."

Arms still crossed, Adder whirled and stalked out of the chamber. Green Ghost sensed someone sidle up next to him. It was Esther. "I think he likes you," she said.

\#

CHAPTER 9

"For the things we have to learn before we can do them, we learn by doing them."
Aristotle

0921 hours, September 25, 2012
Aboard the Roald Amundsen *in the Red Sea*

Green Ghost leaned against the far bulkhead with arms crossed. Some of the Zombies were sleeping in their fold-out bunks, while others sprawled around the spacious hold in chairs and on the floor, listening to their mission briefings and Tactical Insertion Personnel Submarine operating instructions. Tomorrow they'd begin practicing in the actual subs, although it was impossible to actually launch them. Someone came up beside him, but Green Ghost kept his eyes fixed on the man inside the submarine chamber who was already familiarizing himself with the controls: Adder.

"What do you think of that guy?" It was the tall man named Judge.

Instead of answering, Green Ghost asked a question instead. "Would you serve on his team?" He cut his eyes to see Judge's expression.

"That's the question I just asked you, only reworded a little."

"Yeah, but I'm in charge. You first."

Judge had a wide mouth and a chin to match, with a small cleft in the center. He rubbed that with the tip of his forefinger and took a few seconds to answer. "He's an asshole, and probably a real prick to work for... but yeah, if you put me on his team, I'd work with him. I'm not sure what makes him so anti-social, but Adder's proven to me he's a damned hard worker. Look at him right now. He takes the team seriously, so yeah, I could serve under him, although I'd have to see him under fire to say if I'd *keep* doing it. So now it's your turn."

"Thanks for being straight with me," Green Ghost said, then turned back to watching Adder.

"Hey, c'mon, man, don't be like that. I know you're the boss, but I won't tell anybody, and you did promise."

Green Ghost nodded. "I did," he said. "And that was a mistake. I can't afford to answer questions like that. Sorry."

Judge surprised him by laughing low in his throat. "Good answer, boss."

11:50 hours, September 25, 2012
Aboard the Roald Amundsen *at sea*

The mission seemed pretty straightforward, which was what worried Green Ghost. It was the simple missions that always seemed to get fucked up, and this was the simplest. The Zombies would leave the ship using five of the odd-shaped submarines as they steamed past their target islands. The ship would slow to four knots to let them get away, and from that point the clock was ticking. They would have four hours to complete the mission before dawn broke.

With a top speed of eight knots, the submarines would take approximately half an hour to reach the smallest of the three islands, and another half hour to reach the middle one. They would leave all five submarines under guard there, while the rest of the team carried out the mission. Once finished, they would submerge and return to the shipping channel, where homing beacons would lead them to a second ship outfitted with the same underwater airlock system as the *Roald Amundsen.*

Leaning against a fold-out desk affixed to the bulkhead, arms crossed, Green Ghost waited for the other fourteen Zombies to gather close enough to hear him speak over the thrumming of the engines. Despite the nausea welling in his stomach, he refused to let outward signs of seasickness show on his face, especially since some of his team had to have been SEALS. He'd be damned if he let any Navy assholes see him feeling sick. So instead of a grimace, he scowled, making all of the other Zombies wonder what had pissed him off. Now if he just didn't puke all over the deck.

"Is that everybody?" he said once he was certain that it was. The engine noise wasn't all that loud, but it was deep, so he had to pitch his voice higher so it didn't get lost. "Good. You've all had plenty of time to learn the mission details; are there any questions? Speak now..."

Adder raised his finger. Green Ghost's expression didn't change but in his mind he cursed the man.

"The exfil seems sketchy," he said. "We're getting picked up by a second ship?"

"That's the plan."

"I don't like it. Too many moving parts."

"I'll let you tell Saint after we get back."

That brought a couple of chuckles that darkened Adder's face. "I'm telling *you*, as the leader of this mission, that I think it's a bad exfiltration strategy."

Green Ghost didn't answer right away. He hoped Adder would believe that Green Ghost was thinking about what he'd said, when really he was trying not to projectile vomit on the man's feet. Fortuitously the nausea passed quickly. Then he motioned Adder to one side and whispered in his ear.

"Between you and me, I think you're right. But it's too late to change the plan now, so the only thing publicly acknowledging that fact will do is make everybody else doubt the mission."

It was Adder's turn to speak into Ghost's ear. "Is there at least a Plan B?" Adder said. Then they switched positions again.

"Other than swimming? No, but if you think of one, I'll for damned sure implement it."

"How about I scout for boats once we're on the island?"

"Don't get distracted from the primary."

"Not a chance."

Once they'd returned to the group, Green Ghost outlined the organization they would use. As he'd told Angriff, there would be five sections of three people each. He would lead the First Section, with Vapor and Wingnut, and they would be the initial assault element. Adder would have the second section, along with Nimcha and One-Eye, and would be on First Section's left flank. On the right flank would be Third Section, headed by Judge, with Gomorrah and Esther. Fourth Section would be in immediate reserve halfway between the strike elements and the submarines, ready to reinforce either forward at the compound or back where they grounded the subma-rines, in case those were discovered. It would be led by Frosty and also have Zeus and Hili. Lastly, Fifth Section would guard their only way of exfiltration, the submarines, with Claw as Section Leader, and Donner and Pain as Five Two and Five Three.

When Green Ghost announced that Frosty would be the leader of Fourth Section, he studied their faces for signs of disapproval. Females in spe-cial forces teams were virtually unknown, except for special missions, so taking orders from one in the field could have been a problem. But if anyone re-sented her, they hid it well.

"Those call signs sound awfully American," Es-ther said after he'd finished.

Green Ghost nodded in agreement. "We'll change that in future ops, but this dropped in our laps before all the protocols were in place. Plus, a lot of special ops teams run with similar call signs, in-cluding mercs. We'll be good for now."

They would use a variety of Russian firearms fa-vored by *Spetsnaz*, the Russian equivalent of Army Rangers, with about 1,000 or so trained up to the level of SEAL Deltas. Each section would carry the AKM, a modernized version of the AK-47, like the one Green Ghost had used in Mogadishu. A second member of each section would carry an AKM with a GP-25 grenade launcher attached, while the third member hefted a VSS Vintorez silenced sniper rifle. That last gun fired a particularly heavy 9x39mm round which devastated anything it hit, although it gave up some accuracy at very long range. Still, it had become a favored *Spetsnaz* weapon in recent years and could throw off anyone trying to track down Steyer's killers. As a sidearm, they all carried the Russian-made GSh-18 9mm pistol, with an 18-round magazine. Using the right ammunition, those rounds could penetrate most body armor.

Each Zombie would carry four Chinese-made hand grenades, taken from a shipment intended for Iran but intercepted by another US special ops team. Other equipment, including flares, smoke grenades, and body armor, came from various sources hostile to the United States. The only American-manufactured items were their night vision goggles, the performance of which no other country in the world could match.

Camp Zippo, Djibouti
2210 hours, September 28, 2012

"I don't know how you can drink that stuff," Norm Fleming said, pointing with his beer bottle at the half-filled whiskey glass in Angriff's hand.

"If you can only drink one brand of beer, then I can only drink one brand of whiskey."

As if to underscore his point, Angriff picked up the bottle of Rebel Yell and added a splash to his glass. Opportunities to relax and sip whiskey only came rarely for America's top Army officers in Africa. Even at such a late hour, the office beyond Angriff's door buzzed with the business of running a major headquarters.

For such old friends, there was no need for small talk, so they drank in silence until Angriff's phone buzzed.

"That can't be good," Fleming said.

"Not at this time of night." Angriff pushed the

button that connected him to the officer on duty in the outer office. "What is it?"

"Sir, it's General Steeple on the secure line."

Angriff's lifted eyebrow expressed his surprise. Why was the Chairman of the Joint Chiefs calling him? This couldn't be good. He and the new Chief of the General Staff had only met a few times and didn't really know each other. He lifted the phone receiver and was thankful he'd only just started sipping his first drink. "General Steeple, how may I help you?"

"Good evening, Nick. I hope you had not already turned in."

"No, sir, not at all. General Fleming and I were just going over a few things."

"Please give him my regards. I'm calling to check on the progress of our latest project. Several people were asking about it."

"Everything is on schedule, General."

"Have there been any changes to the itinerary, or the guest list?"

"No, sir."

"Good... that's very good. There are important people watching how well you manage this party, Nick. Make sure it goes well."

"I always do, General Steeple."

"Please, call me Tom. I know it's late there, so I'll let you go now. Keep me in the loop."

"Will do, General."

When he'd hung up, Angriff leaned back and took a watery sip from his whiskey.

"What did Steeple want?" Fleming said.

Angriff pursed his lips and thought a moment. "I have no idea."

#

CHAPTER 10

"Why don't I come up and see you sometime when
you're in the nude... I mean mood?"
Shemp Howard

2317 hours, September 30, 2012
Aboard the Roald Amundsen *at sea*

Gearing up had been easy. It was what the
Zombies did best, who they all were at their cores,
warriors ready to fight. There was no modesty
among them, either, because in the teams there
were no sexes; there were only good guys and bad
guys. When Frosty, Donner, and Esther stood nude
and toweled off after a final shower, nobody gave
them a second look.

Repeated run-throughs of the launch procedure
couldn't prepare them for the reality of water flood-
ing the lock around them. Sigurd stood by the digi-
tal panel with two other crewmen, working the various controls. As they sat strapped into their seats in
the submarines, the Zombies could all watch the
cloudy salt water filling up the lock outside the thick
glass walls.

Green Ghost went through the pre-launch
checklist, turning on various systems and checking
monitoring gauges. Since every system was electric,
including the motors for all fans and engines, the

only noise was a low hum. Every time he glanced up at the rising water level, he quickly averted his eyes.

"Is this bothering you, G.G.?" Vapor said.

"No," he lied, in a tone that made it seem ridiculous. In truth, being immersed in the ocean scared him more than people shooting at him did.

"Bullshit, you're as scared as I am."

"These things are cleared to a depth of almost two hundred feet and we're not going anywhere close to that. What's to be scared about?"

"I can think of a dozen things."

The water level rose quickly. Sigurd and his men, safe in the ship's hold, became distorted more than they had been by the two barriers of glass. Then, without warning, a sunshine-yellow fish with two sky blue stripes, one near the head and the other behind the dorsal fin, swam past the cockpit. The light of the ship reflected off its skin in iridescent shimmers that appeared psychedelic. Green Ghost and Vapor broke out laughing at a fish swimming where they'd stood only minutes before. Vapor turned to see Wingnut's reaction, which was nothing more than his usual blank expression.

"C'mon, man, you don't think that's funny?"

For ten seconds the two men stared at each other. Wingnut finally answered. "Hilarious."

"Is he dead?" Vapor said, pointing with his thumb.

"He's a Zombie. As long as he does his job, I don't care if he's dead or alive."

The submarines rested on a heavy steel floor compartmented into five segments. Once the chamber had filled with water and the RPM gauge reached the correct level, the *Roald Amundsen* crewmen working the controls shoved a lever forward that dropped the flooring from beneath Green Ghost's submarine. Dampened by hydraulics and hinged on one side, the door moved until it pointed at a ninety-degree angle downward from the ship's bottom.

The submarine sank until it cleared the ship. Despite the *Roald Amundsen* having slowed to four knots, the submarine was immediately swept backward in the current. In response, Green Ghost's well-practiced movements were automatic. He engaged the gears with one hand while steering with the other. When the engines came online with a *thump* that shook the vessel, he pushed forward on the throttle and then studied the gauges, paying particular attention to the battery level, depth gauge, electromagnetic log, and yoke, which controlled the hydroplanes. The EM read 10 knots, but Green Ghost held the wheel turned twenty degrees right just to compensate for the current. After the longest twenty seconds he could remember, the submarine picked up speed as it cleared the wake of the *Roald Amundsen.*

The stopwatch function on Green Ghost's watch showed three hours, fifty-five minutes left before they had to return for pickup. After allowing enough time for all five subs to clear the ship, he engaged the talk-between-ships short-range radio network. Each of them had microphones attached to their helmets, but those relied on satellites to bounce the signals and the seawater blocked that. He called for a radio check and the other four all responded ready.

"Clock's ticking, people," he said. "Remember

the rules of engagement... if it walks and talks inside that compound, it's fair game, but Steyer and his mistress are the high value targets. And if we're not back for pickup in three hours fifty-four minutes and nine seconds, then we're all fucked."

"Rock on," Vapor said after he muted the microphone.

The run-in took fifty-two minutes to travel six miles, despite the EM showing a consistent speed of ten knots, a speed that should have allowed them to get there in half the time. The plan called for them to run submerged to the western side of the middle of the three islands, Jiftūn aş Şaquīr. A narrow deep-water channel ran on that island's south side and led to a lagoon that would allow them to stay submerged nearly to the beach.

Once there, they would decide the best way to access the small island with the compound on it, Juzur Abū Minqār. The preferred route would be to cross a natural causeway connecting the two islands. The latest satellite photos showed it covered by very shallow water of two feet or less, but if that intelligence proved incorrect, they could use the submarines to land directly on the target. That carried a much higher risk of premature discovery, however, and Green Ghost prayed it wouldn't come to that.

It didn't.

Section Five stayed behind to guard their only realistic exfiltration option, the submarines, while Section Four followed the other sections forward to assault the compound if necessary. If everything went to shit and Section Five was needed, they were in deep reserve.

The distance from their landing spot on the

beach at Jiftūn aş Şaquīr to the eastern spit of sand marking Juzur Abū Minqār was about three-quarters of a mile. Tides were low, as expected, and they crossed the narrow spine of coral and sand with barely a foot of water covering it. The lapping of waves covered any splashing sounds they made.

According to the recon and satellite photos in their mission briefing files, the compound sat very near the eastern shore of Juzur Abū Minqār, on what passed for high ground. Its irregular shape reminded Green Ghost of nothing more than blood spatter, being roughly ovoid with two right angles and numerous curves. An eight-foot cinder-block wall surrounded the compound, with the main gate located on the western side and a one-hundred-foot driveway leading through double iron gates to the interior. At the foot of the driveway was a dock, where intelligence photos had showed a small yacht, a sailing boat, and a 200-ton fast Egyptian patrol boat moored. Until Frosty and her section neared the dock, they wouldn't know whether those boats or others, or any at all, were tied up there.

Three small maintenance entrances ringed the outer wall, each closed by steel doors that were believed to be more discouragement for potential intruders than actual barriers. But there was only one way to find out for sure how strong they were, and that was by trying to get through them.

One sentry stood guard on a raised platform so he could see east, along the exact path the Zombies used to approach. With NVGs in place, Green Ghost motioned for them to halt. Then he held up his left hand, palm facing forward with all of the Zombies behind him. Using his index finger, he pointed up twice, the gesture for *look up*, then used the same finger to indicate one sentry. Since Section One was in the lead, he pointed at Wingnut, the designated sniper in his three-man section. There were no secrets in a team that had trained as closely in the past weeks as TFZ, and all of them knew that Green Ghost was far and away the best shot among them. Nor was he falsely modest enough to argue the point. He'd given Wingnut the sniper rifle because he had confidence in the man, and so that he could then concentrate on leading.

Darkness hid the Zombies, as no lights shone much beyond the compound wall. Wingnut showed no hesitation. At a range of 200 yards and with no more emotion than he typically showed, he sighted the rifle and pulled the trigger. The silenced metallic cough made less noise than a small wave breaking on the shore. The guard had been leaning forward on his elbows when the round struck him in the forehead. His head jerked backward and then flopped forward again, leaving him draped over the wall's top.

Now they had to move fast. With the eastern shoreline so close to the rear compound wall, something that hadn't been visible in the satellite photos, there was no need for a ready reserve to cover their fallback.

"Four One, new plan. Circle the wall to the left and cut any retreat to the boat docks. You've got two mikes before we go in, unless the Egyptians discover their dead buddy and we start the party early, then it's your decision on how to proceed. No change in timing."

Four One was Frosty, with Zeus and Hili in her section.

"Got it, One One. Nobody gets out alive, not on

my watch."

"Two One, your section blows the door. Mine goes through, then you follow, taking the left flank. Three One, you've got wall security until we're both inside, then you follow and take the right. Go."

C-4 had been chosen as the plastic explosive for the mission because of its ubiquitous global use. Nobody could trace it back to the USA, and the blocks they carried had been captured during the interdiction of a shipment to North Korea, so all of the writing was in Korean. One-Eye moved forward with a brick of C-4 and, using a knife, cut the paper surround away from the pure white material. He molded it around the heavy push-down latch, and then used two more bricks pushed into the cracks between the wall and the door near the hinges. Without knowing the door's thickness or strength, it was necessary to make sure they used enough explosives to get through on the first go. Three bricks of C-4 were enough to blow a hole through the wall itself.

After inserting the detonator, he retreated to a shallow depression near the beach with the rest of them. Instead of a remote control, they used a hard-wired detonator, just to eliminate any chance of interference with the signal. Green Ghost stared at his watch as the last seconds ticked off until Frosty and her people were supposed to be in place.

At two minutes he spoke into his microphone. "Four One, are you in position?"

There was a short delay before she answered in a whisper. "Roger that, One One. Two guards down. There are three boats here, but one is Egyptian Navy with crew on watch. Do we take them out, too?"

Fuck!

"Can you neutralize it, Four One?"

"I've got an idea, One One. Give me two more minutes."

"No more. We're cutting this too close as it is."

After warning her at fifty seconds, Green Ghost again spoke. "Time's up."

"Blow it."

One-Eye watched him for the blast signal. The detonator had been home built so as not to give away any traceable evidence. At ten seconds, Green Ghost pointed and One-Eye pushed the firing button, while they all rolled into a ball for protection. The ensuing blast knocked the steel door inward as if a hurricane wind drove it, while metal shards and debris showered them. Two seconds later, Green Ghost was up and running to be first through the shattered doorway, with Vapor and Wingnut right on his heels.

Directly ahead, past an Olympic-sized swimming pool, rose the main house, two stories with lots of glass, and two wings on either side connected by covered passageways. A narrow causeway crossed the pool, which had a dozen covered cabanas encircling it like those at a posh resort. Lighting at that time of night was dim, with most of the inside lights also turned off. Few people inside were awake when the C-4 went off.

But that didn't last long.

The dock had concrete pilings and wood planking. Two small civilian cabin cruisers lay moored on the southern side, but those didn't concern Frosty nearly as much as the 62-ton Egyptian Navy *Komar*-class patrol boat tied off on the northern side. It wasn't the 200-ton monster visible on the intel photos, and their briefing packet had mentioned that such boats might be in the area, and while they were old Soviet-era craft, they remained dangerous to small submarines and merchant vessels. Aside from two missiles, it also had a twin 25mm gun mount on the bow. With a top speed of more than 40 knots, it posed a mortal threat to their exfiltration plans. The boat had to be put out of action, but a bored guard stood at the bow facing the main house, probably wishing he was sleeping inside.

"One One, this is Four One," she whispered into the mike.

"Go, Four One."

"There's an Egyptian missile boat moored at the dock, along with two civilian craft."

"Can you neutralize it, Four One?"

Frosty turned her head away, eyes flicking between Zeus and Hili, thinking. Moonlight reflected on the close-cropped white blonde hair that gave her her name.

"I've got an idea, One One. Give me two more minutes."

"No more. We're cutting this too close as it is."

She motioned Zeus and Hili in close and whispered rather than use the mike. "Give me your C-4 bricks and a detonator. C'mon, hurry it up. Hili, at my signal, take down that guard. Once I blow this stuff, Zeus, you put grenades into those two civvy boats, got it?"

"What are you gonna do, boss?"

Instead of answering, she crawled closer to the Egyptian missile boat and then pointed backward at Hili. One silenced round put the guard down on deck. She sprinted fifty feet down the beach to the point nearest the boat's bow and then waded into the water, thigh deep, until she could touch the hull. Working as fast as she dared, Frosty cut off the paper, peeled back the strip attached to the glue panel on one side, and fixed all three bricks to the boat's hull about a foot above the waterline. There was no swell and the hull was clean enough for them to stick.

"How's my time?" she whispered into her mike.

"Fifty seconds," answered Green Ghost.

Running the detonator through the first two into the side of the third, she backed out of the water, letting the thin metal detonating wire unspool behind her. She'd nearly made it back to Zeus and Hili when Green Ghost spoke again.

"Time's up."

"Blow it."

#

CHAPTER 11

"Courage in danger is half the battle."
Plautus

0028 hours, October 1, 2012
Jazāir Jiftūn Island, Egypt

Even as Green Ghost led the way across the pool using the causeway, Adder's Section Two came in on the left. Adder cleared out two uniformed Egyptian soldiers with two shots, while Nimcha moved straight toward the left building, rifle at his shoulder and eye on the scope. One-Eye set up on one knee to cover both of them from any shots from the balcony that ringed the second floor. Three seconds after he'd set up the VSS Vintorez, three half-dressed Egyptians stumbled out of an upstairs doorway. He dropped two but missed the third, who fell to his stomach and shot back. The hastily aimed rounds went high and wide until the man raised his head three inches to get a better angle. It was all One-Eye needed to blow off the top of his head.

Although she was expecting it, the blast from the rear of the compound caught Frosty by surprise. She flinched before triggering the detonator switch. The ensuing blast rocked the Egyptian missile boat, blowing the bow sideways with such force that it ripped a mooring stanchion away from the dock in a shower of wood splinters. Unable to continue sideways, the thwarted energy rocked the boat and forced the bow down, into the water, where it poured into the hull from the five-foot hole in its metal skin.

Several crewmen stumbled on deck, unable to stand as the boat rocked beneath them. One man moved toward the twin 25mm guns and a second staggered upright, holding a rifle. Both fell as Frosty and Hili gunned them down. Zeus sprang from their position and walked down the dock, firing 40mm grenades into the cabins of the other two ships. One caught fire immediately, while the other sparked and hissed from ruined electronics. A third Egyptian on the missile boat aimed at his exposed back but fell with two rounds through his neck, courtesy of Hili.

Within two minutes, the missile boat rested on the bottom in two feet of water, giving the boat a thirty degree down-angle at the bow. For the time being, no other crewmen came on deck.

"Dock secured," she said into the mike. "All boats neutralized."

Green Ghost heard explosions on both sides as One-Eye and Gomorrah, who both had the grenade-launcher equipped AKMs, fired them into the side buildings. Another, much louder detonation came from the other side of the main house and he knew Frosty had done her job.

Gunfire broke out all around him. As he stepped off the causeway and back onto the concrete surrounding the pool, he felt something slam into his chest and knock him half a step back. But even as the bullet struck him, he'd been shifting aim to the man standing in a sliding doorway on his left and he had the chance to fire. His shot also hit home and the half-naked Egyptian, who wasn't wearing body armor, bent back, fell to his knees, and toppled forward.

Vapor moved up beside him, knelt, and fired two three-round bursts into the double glass doors leading inside. Once the ruptured glass had fallen away, he fired a 40mm grenade into the darkened room beyond, turning away at the moment of blast. Screams followed.

"G.G., you okay?"

"Yeah, go, make entry. And call me One One."

Although the Egyptian round hadn't penetrated his body armor, it felt like he'd been slammed with a baseball bat. Gasping through the pain of breathing in the lungfuls of air he needed to keep going, he followed Vapor through the broken glass glittering on the patio and into the house.

In the halls and room of such a large house, it was impossible to know what was going on around him. Narrowing down the exact location of the shots and explosions proved impossible. As he followed Vapor across a huge room with a central fireplace in its center, with openings on all four sides and chairs crowded around a flat-screen TV on one wall, it was his job to secure Vapor's rear. An errant round had hit the middle of the TV screen but somehow it still worked. A soccer game played over the shattered shards, like a moving Piccaso painting.

Speed was the key to the assault. Green Ghost

had realized immediately that they were up against Egyptian regulars, probably Muslim Brotherhood members but trained troops regardless of their affiliation. Unlike US troops, however, who were trained for individual initiative, the Egyptian Army relied more on their officers for orders. Unquestioning obedience to orders was the most important element, and without specific orders they ran into hallways and rooms and went down under the Americans' bullets. Green Ghost and Vapor reached the foyer under double curving stairways that led to the second floor, leaving a trail of six bodies in their wake.

"Two One, sitrep?"

"Left wing cleared. We're moving down the hallway to the main house. No sign of either HVT."

"Roger that. We're in entry hall, waiting to move upstairs. Three One, report?"

"Right building cleared. We've got some phones, notebooks, and other intel. Three NCs."

"Servants?"

"More like hookers. What do we do with them?"

Damn, damn, damn! Orders were to leave no witnesses, but how could he order his people to murder innocent civilians?

"One One, this is Three Two. I've got an idea." Three Two was Gomorrah.

"I'm listening."

"I speak Arabic. I'm going to tell them we're Austrian *jagdkommandos* come to clean up Steyer, who used to be one of us."

"Nobody's gonna believe that."

"Muddies the waters."

He only hesitated for a second. "Do it, then zip ties and gags. Then move on the main house."

"Can do. We're on our way."

Hallways leading to the two wings entered the foyer on both sides. Within a minute Adder stood in one archway, flanked by Nimcha and One-Eye. Using hand gestures, Green Ghost asked if he could see what awaited them on the landing above and Adder gestured yes, four riflemen and a light machine gun. Seconds later, Judge and Gomorrah showed up in the hallway to the left of the front doors. Once again using hand signals, he told both teams to use their grenade launchers to fire at the top of the stairway opposite their position. Adder indicated they only had one round left, so Green Ghost told Adder that when the others fired, he should move out from directly under the landing above and put a grenade straight up. Holding up three fingers so they could all see his hand, he counted down. Three... two... one... fire!

In perfect synchronization, they put four grenades onto the landing, after which Adder, Judge, and Green Ghost followed with direct rifle fire. One of the Egyptians fell over the railing onto the tile floor of the foyer. Adder went up one stairway with Nimcha behind him and One-Eye staying below to secure the entrance. Green Ghost, Judge, and Gomorrah went up the other. Three mangled bodies littered the landing, where a huge oil painting of some bearded guy in a black robe hung askew on the wall, with dozens of shrapnel tears in the canvas. More hallways led off to either side. No words were necessary for them to split off in each direction, but Green Ghost paused as Frosty spoke on their network intercom.

"One One, this is Four One. We've got company, unknown aircraft headed this way."

"Fixed wing?"

"Negative. Helicopter."

Damn, damn, damn!

"Where the hell did they come from?" Zeus said.

All three Zombies had flipped down their NVGs as the helicopter came their way fast.

"That's a Sea King," Hili said. "I've flown on birds like that a hundred times."

"Armed?"

"Nothing organic, but who knows how they could've modified it? Probably carrying troops."

They had repositioned back on the side of the dock behind one of the concrete pillars, right where the beach sloped down to the waterline. Frosty raised her head for a better look at the approaching aircraft and drew fire from the missile boat that chewed up the wood near her face. One splinter hit her left jaw and left a bloody smear.

"Shit."

Her brain calculated the situation in seconds. The AKMs fired a 7.62 x 39mm round instead of the later Russian AK-74s, which only shot a 5.45 x 39mm cartridge, but even the larger bullet wouldn't do excessive damage to such a large helicopter. Worse, while men on the missile boat pinned them down, they couldn't do more than snipe short bursts at the incoming helicopter. They needed more fire-power...

"Either one of you know how to operate that gun?" she said, indicating the Type 61 25mm gun mount on the missile boat. The two multi-purpose cannon lined up one on top of the other, instead of side by side. *Those* guns could drive the helicopter away if they didn't shoot it down first.

"I saw it done once," answered Zeus. "Simple stuff, the trigger is right behind the gun. The traverse is done by hand controls... I think it's mostly hydraulic." Then he paused, realized what she had in mind, and nodded. "Cover me, on three."

"Negative! This is on me."

Without waiting, she jumped to her feet and ran for the boat, her feet slipping in the crushed coral and sand of the beach. Bullets kicked up around her until Zeus and Hili opened fire on automatic. Halfway to the beached missile boat, the deck itself blocked any further fire coming from on board.

Wading out for a second time, she saw the effect of the C-4 blast up close. A round hole more than five feet across had blackened and fire-smoothed edges. Strips of metal pushed inward by the explosion ringed the opening like jagged teeth, but she could only see half of the hole. The rest was under water.

The missile boat's freeboard had been a daunting six feet before it sank. Putting the rifle sling around her neck, Frosty was able to grab the deck's handrail and pull herself up, only to draw immediate rifle fire. She dropped back over the edge, hanging on with one hand and swinging like a monkey with her lower legs in the water. The shooter appeared to be hiding behind the gun turret she intended to use, which was twenty feet back from the prow.

Without hesitating, she took a Chinese fragmentation grenade off her belt. The grenade used a standard ring-and-safety lever design, but holding the grenade and pulling the pin required two hands. Unlike in the movies, she couldn't use her teeth to pull out the pin. It required too much force. But while hanging there, she couldn't use both hands, either.

The blast hole offered the solution. Using her right hand, the same one holding the grenade, she found a jagged metal strip inside the hole over which she put the pin. Then, with a yank, it came free. The Chinese grenade was supposed to have an eight-second fuse, but at the count of three, she tossed it onto the deck where she hoped the Egyptian was crouched.

Like most grenades, the explosion was small. But inside the Type 82-2 fragmentation grenade were thousands of small steel pellets that acted like buckshot from a shotgun shell. Screams let her know she'd hit the man and she was up and onto the deck within seconds.

He'd been near the turret and was rolling on his back when she got near, hands to his face. Darkness hid the extent of his wounds but it didn't matter. She aimed between his hands and put two rounds into his head.

The turret was open topped, with access through swinging hatches on both sides. Frosty entered through the portside door and settled into the gunner's seat one second before bullets ricocheted from the metal around her. Without conscious thought, she pulled the other frag grenade from her belt, pulled the ring, and tossed it backward over her head with hopes it wouldn't bounce into the water. It landed on the deck with a loud *thunk* that could not be misinterpreted as anything but dangerous.

Seven seconds later, a muffled *whump* indicated the explosive had struck the water and sunk, rendering it harmless. But that didn't matter now, because it had served its purpose. The Egyptian shooter had taken cover and stopped firing, giving Frosty the break she needed. Now, if only the twin guns were loaded...

They were.

Two belts fed into chambers carrying the 25mm rounds. In the darkness she couldn't tell how much ammo she had, or what type ordnance it was, but it looked like a lot of something. Using the foot pedals to rotate the turret, and two hand levers to raise and lower the two cannon barrels, she pointed the gun straight backward toward the boat's small superstructure. The firing button couldn't have been more obvious, being the size of a half-dollar and bright red. Aiming through the large ring sight, she pushed the button.

Nothing happened; there had to be a safety switch, but where? Shadows hid the interior details of the turret, but she couldn't reach the tactical light near the back of her combat belt. Using her heels, she pushed herself upward enough to detach it, exposing her head and shoulders. A three-round burst from an unseen shooter struck her in the sternum, left breast, and shoulder. The impacts slammed her back into the seat, where she slumped out of view.

Red flashes filled her vision. Breaths came with electric pain that radiated down her legs and arms. Something wet and sticky ran down her left side. She should have passed out, but didn't. Instincts kicked in and combat-honed reflexes took over. Turning on the flashlight, she found the safety switch under the column with the firing button. She didn't aim this time, because that involved pushing back up in the seat to use the sight. Instead she pushed the red button.

Bam-bam. Each barrel fired independently, with less than half a second between them. At point-blank range, the 25mm shells ripped through the thin metal of the control room in a shower of sparks and shrapnel, followed by two explosions. Her brain had compartmentalized the pain of her wounds and registered the detonations as evidence of high explosive rounds. Then she fired a second time, and a third. After the last volley, a screaming man dove overboard while the boat's cabin burned behind him.

Mental discipline could only take her so far and as the adrenaline of that initial fight wore off, Frosty pushed against the chair, writhing in pain. She heard the *whang* of more bullets, which brought her back to the present. Where were they coming from? The missile boat was on fire, so that couldn't be it.

Only then did the cyclical *whump* of helicopter blades register on her conscious mind. She no longer saw its running lights and rotated the turret back toward the bow, looking for it. There, hovering thirty feet off the ground and blowing sand in all directions from the wash of its rotors, was the Sea King, with riflemen standing in its open doorway firing at her. Working the controls, she laid the gunsight on the aircraft just as it settled for a landing, and fired six rounds back to back.

Bam-bam, bam-bam, bam-bam.

The first two missed low; the next four hit the men huddled in the doorway, the cockpit, and the fuselage below the rotors. Screams echoed across the beach and the helicopter dropped the final ten feet as the blades dug deep into the sand and coral, wobbled, and toppled on its left side. Fire licked out from the engine compartment and she saw figures crawling in the wreckage.

But blood loss and shock crept up on her without Frosty realizing it. Sparkles filled her vision again and her head lolled backward. Without even realizing it, she pushed the firing button three more times, and then passed out.

#

CHAPTER 12

"I never felt more alive than when I died on a Dacian sword."
Inscription on the tomb of a Roman centurion in Moesia

0059 hours, October 1, 2012
Jazāir Jiftūn Island, Egypt

Upstairs at the main house was laid out with hallways on either side of the landing, with multiple rooms on both sides. The only way to get through them was with one man on rear security, one to open each door, and the third ready to fire the instant a target presented itself. The biggest danger was automatic weapons fire before they could make entry, which was where hand grenades came in.

Green Ghost's section took the right hallway while Adder's took the left. Judge and his people locked down the foyer. The first two rooms Green Ghost checked were empty, but in the third he found a nude, heavy-set man with a graying beard and military haircut standing behind two naked young women. The instant he saw Green Ghost, the man fired four rounds from a pistol, but missed as the Zombie ducked out of the doorway.

"Shit," he said. "The target has human shields."

Vapor and Wingnut exchanged glances and

nods. Vapor spoke for the both of them. "ROEs say no witnesses, G.G."

It was true and he knew it. But it wasn't in Green Ghost's soul to simply murder two non-combatants in cold blood, especially since they'd already spared three servants... or hookers, or whatever they were. Then he thought of something and pointed at Wingnut. "Don't you speak Russian?"

"Polish."

"Close enough. Here's what we do."

After a few seconds outlining his plan, Wingnut called into the room. "Jesteśmy przyjaciółmi." *We're friends.* Given the carnage they had already wrought, it seemed like a stupid thing to say, but the Zombies doubted that the Egyptian women spoke Russian, or knew the difference between Russian and Polish. Wingnut repeated the phrase three times, slowly, so the women would remember. Then he slid the barrel of his rifle through the doorway at ground level, drawing fire from the man within. Simultaneously Green Ghost stepped into the doorway with scope to his eye, located the target's forehead, and squeezed the trigger. One shot, one kill. The fat man collapsed.

None of them spoke, per his instructions, since many Egyptians spoke English and would know an American accent when they heard it. Working quickly, Vapor and Wingnut zip-tied the girls' hands and feet, and then gagged them. Wingnut picked up the dead man's uniform coat with the tip of his rifle and showed it to Green Ghost. Medals weighed it down, but it was the epaulets that caught their attention. All of them recognized the rank, signified by its olive green color, featuring a gold button, the stylized Eagle of Saladin, one star, and crossed scimitars, all in gold thread. The man had been a lieutenant general.

"Anybody got eyes on the target?" he said into the intercom once they were back in the hallway.

"Target is neutralized." It was Adder's voice. "Taking photos now. We've also got the girlfriend."

"On my way."

Leaving Wingnut and Vapor to finish clearing out the floor, he trotted down the other hallway to find Adder standing over the bloody corpse of Alois Steyer in the third room down. At that moment, they all heard the cannonfire from the front of the compound.

"Sounds like we're missing the fun," Adder said. He stood with his pistol aimed at the head of a tall, lean blonde. A hard face had probably once been pretty, Green Ghost thought, but the years had not been kind to Steyer's mistress.

Her eyes flicked from one to the other of them. "You're Americans? Thank God!" she said. "These animals kidnapped me and I couldn't escape."

More cannonfire echoed from the dock area, followed by a loud crash and rifle fire. The Zombies ignored the woman.

"That doesn't sound good," Adder said.

Green Ghost keyed his mike. "Four One, sitrep!"

"One One, this is Four Two. Four One is down and we're under fire from two directions. Request backup immediately."

"What's your position?"

"Four Two and Four Three are at the base of the dock, left side facing the water. Four One is on the boat, in a turret near the front. Boat is on fire. Crew has abandoned ship and is advancing on our position using the dock as cover. Downed helicopter is between us and exfil with active shooters still in the area."

"You've got to get me out of here!" the woman said, grabbing Adder by the elbow.

He jerked his arm away. "You want me to do her?" he said, pointing with his pistol.

"Is your name Williamson?" Green Ghost said. "Holly Williamson?"

For the first time she looked afraid. "How... how did you know that?"

Green Ghost stared at her, searching for any sign of regret at being found with a known arms dealer, any remorse or even recognition of the harm her lover had done. Instead, all he saw in the way her brown eyes roamed from one of them to the other was calculation. She was looking for an opening.

"No," he said to Adder. "I'll do it."

Green Ghost raised his rifle and pointed it between her eyes, and for the first time Holly Williamson realized they knew who she was. Dropping to her knees, she begged them not to kill her. The tears rolling down her face weren't fake this time. Green Ghost tried to pull the trigger, hesitated, then exhaled and tried again. Suddenly he jumped as a pistol went off next to him. Williamson's head snapped back and then she slumped sideways.

"Let's get out of here," Adder said.

"You didn't have to do that," Green Ghost said as they descended the stairway. "It was my responsibility."

"If she wasn't gonna blow us, I didn't see the point in keeping her alive," Adder answered. "Besides, I don't mind getting my hands dirty."

Beyond the heavy wooden double doors at the front of the house was a circular driveway, leading from wrought iron gates centered in the wall on that side of the compound. Smoke and flames rose beyond the wall and they all heard the *pop* of rifle fire.

Gathered in the foyer, Green Ghost counted heads and nodded in satisfaction that all nine Zombies of Sections One, Two, and Three were assembled and without casualties, testament to the tactical value of surprise.

"Five One, can you hear?"

"Hear you fine, One One."

"Sitrep?"

"All quiet on the eastern front. We hear a lot of explosions, One One. Do we move up to reinforce you?"

"Negative. Turn the subs for fast exfil and prepare to assist with casualties."

"Should we expect enemy interdiction?"

"Unknown but assume yes. I will inform you when we're done here. We have at least one casualty. Prep for bullet, shrapnel, or compression wounds. One One out."

The nine Zombies assembled by the front gate. The foot of the dock was ninety feet directly ahead down a crushed coral driveway, with Zeus and Hili pinned down on the left. Beyond them on that side, both civilian boats smoldered. No flames were visible, but in the uncertain light Green Ghost spotted figures with rifles. Opposite those lay the sunken missile boat with the wounded Frosty in the turret, and to their right lay the burning Sea King. That blaze partially illuminated the area but also created dancing shadows that played tricks with their vision and rendered NVGs unuseable. Once he'd spent five seconds assessing the situation, he ducked back behind the wall and tapped Judge on the shoulder.

"I'm going after Frosty. When I move out, you and your section put fire on those bogies near the 'copter."

Adder, Nimcha, and One-Eye were thirty feet away past the open gate, while Wingnut and Vapor crouched behind him. He opened the mike and ordered them to engage the enemy on the dock and in the civilian boats. When that happened, the two men pinned down behind a piling were to run like hell toward the gate. It was a dangerous maneuver, since Hili and Zeus would be running toward their own firing comrades and needed to bear left to provide a clear field of fire. That meant their withdrawal would be a loop, taking that much longer to execute, but there was nothing else to do.

Without any more delay, Green Ghost leapt forward and ran for the missile boat, a distance of roughly forty yards. It took the Egyptians by surprise. For the first second nobody shot at him, and it took two more seconds for them to swing around and track him. In high school, he had briefly run track, because his time in the forty-yard dash had been better than the Tennessee state record, but home life had forced him to quit the team. Now that speed saved his life. By the time the Egyptians could fire, he was at the boat.

Bullets struck the hull around him. After taking a moment to consider pushing through the hole into the boat's interior, he gathered himself to scramble up the side and reached for the deck two feet over his head. That drew immediate rifle fire and he jerked his hand back.

"Cover me," said a voice. It was Adder, who had followed him.

"Stand down! It's my job, not yours."

"I'm bigger than you, Ghost. I can carry her easier than you can, and you're a better shot than me. Just keep those assholes from shooting me in the ass and let's get out of here."

Part of him wanted to force the issue to prove who was in command, but he also realized that Adder was right. Putting ego aside, Green Ghost nodded his agreement.

The closest shooters were across the dock on the civilian boats, but while the Zombies were in the water, they were hidden by the dock itself. Once Adder slung his rifle across his back and used both hands to pull himself up to the deck, he became an easy target. Except Green Ghost flipped down his NVGs, propped his rifle on the edge of the dock, and waited for a shooter to show himself. Right on time, a man stood up on the deck of the boat thirty feet away and Green Ghost put three rounds into his chest. After that he found no other targets, although elsewhere the sounds of battle increased.

"Gimme a hand," Adder yelled over the background shooting. Green Ghost slung his own rifle and Adder passed the unconscious Frosty down to him. Blood soaked the left side of her uniform. Once Adder had also climbed back down, he carried her in his arms at a trot as Green Ghost walked backward, shooting at anything that moved. They got back to the gate without getting hit.

Zeus and Hili made it safely back to the group at the gate. Green Ghost knelt inside the wall to catch his breath, until Nimcha tapped his shoulder and pointed to the western sky. Two small red dots headed their way out of the skyline of white lights that marked the city of Hurghada. The other Zombies noticed and followed his finger.

"Shit," Vapor said. "Another bird."

"Let's get out of here," Green Ghost said into the intercom. "Section One stays here as rear guard. Three One, hold the back door. Section Two, exfil to the subs. Go!"

They had never trained for such an exercise as a team, but the Zombies were the best of the best and it was a basic tactical retreat under fire, spurred on by the reality of the oncoming Egyptian reinforcements. Green Ghost was last to cross the swimming pool in a reversal of his earlier path over the bridge. He was also last to exit through the back door, one second before a fusilade of bullets chewed up the cinder blocks of the wall surrounding it.

At the beach, Green Ghost's Section One took over rear guard from Judge's Section Three, who followed Adder's people back across the watery causeway. Then it was Vapor's turn. Seconds later, Wingnut had slung his rifle and turned to follow them when four figures appeared on the compound wall and opened fire. Bullets zipped around the two remaining Zombies with buzzing *thwip* sounds, but the darkness hid them. Green Ghost returned fire using NVGs and watched two men topple backward before the other two ducked out of sight.

"C'mon, let's go," he said to Wingnut.

"I'm afraid I caught one, Ghost."

"Where?"

"Left thigh."

Green Ghost helped him lie on his stomach in

the sand while he felt the wounded man's thigh, searching for the wound. He found it where blood pumped out around his fingers.

"What are you guys doing?" Vapor said, having come back at the sound of rifle fire.

"He's hit. Keep 'em off that wall while I stop the bleeding."

"Just carry him, G.G. We've gotta scram."

"He'll bleed out."

"Fuck."

"Sorry to inconvenience you," Wingnut said with obvious pain in his voice. It was the most they had ever heard him say at one time.

Green Ghost stuck the tactical light in his mouth as he worked, making himself a perfect target in the dark. Vapor fired several times but he ignored the shots. All of the Zombies carried a medical kit and had extensive training in stopping bleeds in the field, since excessive bleeding was the main killer on the battlefield. First he applied a combat tourniquet around Wingnut's thigh, and then applied Woundstat granules followed by combat gauze. Because the man's leg was so wide, he used up all of both his and Wingnut's gauze. Only when he finished, a minute after starting, did he hear the enemy rifle fire. Hoisting the semi-conscious Wingnut over his shoulders, he stood, shifted the weight until it was equally divided, and started across the causeway.

"Let's gitfoh!"

0116 hours, October 1, 2012

Despite superior numbers, the Egyptians didn't follow them into the night, but their second helicopter did. The Zombies had all boarded their submarines and were headed out into water deep enough to submerge when the aircraft finally discovered them, using a high-powered searchlight beam. There wasn't enough time for them to circle back as the American craft disappeared under water.

At a depth of thirty feet, the only light inside the submarines were the dim red gauge lights. From above, Green Ghost knew they were invisible and, thanks to the electric motors, there were no bubble trails to follow. From there it was only a matter of meeting their pickup ship. So far they'd been damned lucky, with two badly wounded but no KIAs, although both Frosty and Wingnut could still die if they didn't reach a medical facility soon.

"How is he?" Green Ghost asked as the submarine ran without the underwater headlamps on into the dark waters of the Red Sea.

"I think you stopped the bleeding, but he lost a lot of blood. He's not looking good, G.G."

"Yeah."

It took fifty-six minutes to reach the rendevous point. Green Ghost periodically shut down the air conditioning. Running the engines at full speed the entire time drained the batteries at an alarming rate and dead batteries meant dead Zombies. After what seemed like hours, they arrived at the rendevous coordinates. There was no way to know if the Egyptian helicopter was still up there, except to surface, and so, with the wounded Zombies needing immediate medical attention, he did.

Sweat dripped off his nose as Green Ghost's submarine broke the surface. He undogged the hatch and fresh air flooded into the cabin, warm and moist with the smell of brine. Standing with his upper torso outside the boat, he used the Russian infrared binoculars to scan for their pickup ship. All around, the other submarines broke the surface, too.

As the little submersible bobbed in the choppy sea, he saw nothing. There was no sign of the Egyptian helicopter or their safe-haven home. The plan called for the merchantman, named the *Athena* and crewed by South Africans with a flag out of Malta, to arrive at 0215 hours, pretend to have engine trouble, and then wait for them until 0330 hours. Had it been delayed somehow? He didn't know, but their wounded needed medical help ASAP. Using his right index finger, he flipped open a small hinged door on the instrument panel and pushed the red button inside.

#

Chapter 13

"One man with courage makes a majority."
General Andrew Jackson

0237 hours, October 3, 2012
Camp Zippo, Djibouti

Angriff drew on his cigar, unaware that a night breeze blew the smoke back toward Norm Fleming. "The stars are never brighter than under a desert night," he said.

Fleming waved his hand in front of his nose. "I'm surprised you can see them."

"Eh? Is it bothering you?"

"If I smoked, it wouldn't."

"But you *don't* smoke."

"That is true."

Although he'd only smoked a third of it, Angriff snuffed it out in the sand and used a pocket knife to trim away the charred section. Cigars never tasted as good when you relit them after trimming, but getting more Cuban Monte Cristo Especiales Number Threes in the Horn of Africa was iffy at best.

"Thank you," Fleming said.

"You *do* know I've already got a wife, right?"

Fleming grinned, his white teeth fairly gleaming in the moonlight. "I think I've met her two or a thousand times. You married way over your head."

"Great, now you even sound like her."

"One thing we would agree on. Janine would not believe you came out here to admire the stars any more than I do."

"I can't just sit in there and stare at the radio." He pointed with his thumb at the pre-fabricated metal building fifty feet to the east. "I'm not good at waiting."

"You did everything you could to ensure their safety, but you're not their father. They're professionals, they know what they're doing, and they know the score. You picked the right leader, you gave them everything they needed to accomplish the mission, and they're—"

"General Angriff!"

The two generals turned to see Corporal Raegar standing in the headquarters doorway, peering into the dark desert.

"General, is that you?"

"On our way, Corporal," Angriff said.

More than fifty people worked in the PCC, meaning things were tight. If your dinner had garlic in it, everybody knew. So when Angriff stepped through the doorway he instantly knew something had gone wrong. All faces turned toward him, and then quickly turned away. Leaning over the shoulder of an E-3 clicking away at a computer keyboard, staring at the man's monitor, was Major Rip Kordibowsky.

"It's not good, sir," Kordibowsky said as Angriff drew near.

But Fleming, as the Head of Operations, answered. "Be succinct, Major."

Kordibowsky addressed Fleming. "Green Ghost activated his emergency warning signal."

"Position?"

The major leaned down to better see the computer screen. "It looks to be in the middle of the shipping channel, maybe seven miles east of the littlest island. Right where he's supposed to be."

"Where's the pick-up ship?" Angriff said.

"That's the *Athena,* General, she's..." Once again he bent and peered at the screen, and said something to the woman sitting before it. She clacked a few keys. It took a few seconds before Kordibowsky stood, his face reflecting obviously bad news. "The *Athena* is four miles north of the rendevous, proceeding at eight knots in the direction of Suez."

Throughout the headquarters, voices dropped as the staff working that late at night turned, ears cocked for details of what was obviously a crisis. Fleming noticed.

"Get me the ship's captain, Rip," Angriff said. "Get him now!"

"Nick." Fleming cast his voice low and motioned toward the eavesdropping staff with his head.

Angriff stuck the butt of the cigar into his mouth, biting down hard on the end. He scowled at the others, who busied themselves doing something else. "Send that call into my office."

Angriff stared out the window as they waited for the call to go through.

"I've got a bad feeling about this," he said.

"We don't know anything yet."

"Where the hell's that captain?"

As if in answer, a face materialized on the computer screen on his desk. A man in his thirties wearing a blue shirt was talking, but it took a few seconds before his voice came through. He had a

South African accent. "...the captain will be very sorry he missed your call, General."

"Who are you?"

The man seemed surprised. "As I said, General, I'm *Athena*'s Chief Mate, Adem de Haan. Captain Vinke is tied up with an urgent problem in the engine room and will be very sorry he missed your call."

Angriff studied the man's face for nearly twenty seconds, watching his muscles twitch and his eyes blink. The longer he stared, the brighter red the man's face became. Then he nodded slightly; the man was lying.

"I don't like liars, de Haan, especially not when they're supposed to be on my side."

"I... don't know what you mean, General."

"At this moment, there are four unmanned aerial vehicles flying 3,000 feet above your ship, Mr. de Haan, and *you* are about to be their target. Each one carries four Hellfire missiles capable of doing great damage to your ship. Tell Captain Vinke he has thirty seconds to join this call or they fire those missiles. They might not sink your ship, but they will sure as hell make it burn."

"But he is in the engine room! I cannot reach him that quickly."

"Twenty-eight seconds."

The man ducked out of sight.

"Drones?" Fleming said with raised eyebrows.

Angriff dropped his voice and leaned out of the camera's view. "He doesn't know I'm bluffing."

Another face came into view. A white beard and close-cropped white hair framed the tanned face of Captain Vinke. He wore his uniform hat, and Angriff wondered if he'd put it on to impress the general. If so, it hadn't worked.

"What's this about shooting at us?" the captain said.

"If you don't turn your ship around right now, Vinke, that's exactly what I'm going to do!"

"I wish you people would make up your mind. Not two hours ago, you told me *not* to proceed with our agreed-upon plan and to make my way through the canal. Now you're threatening me! What's going on over there?"

"I didn't tell you any such thing!"

"Not you, no, it was your government!"

Angriff leaned back, squinting. Adrenaline poured into his veins and heat rose up his throat. He stuck the unlit cigar into his jaw in a conscious effort to hide his shock and turned toward Fleming, arching his eyebrows with the unspoken question whether he knew anything about this. Out of the line of sight, Fleming shook his head and mouthed *no.*

"That's not how this works," Angriff finally said. "You take your orders from *me*, and only me. And my government doesn't directly intervene in active operations, so try again, Vinke. Tell me what really happened, and do it fast!"

"You can yell all you want, General. It won't change the facts. I received a personal call from someone very high up in your government who ordered me to leave those men behind, and also not to divulge their identity on pain of punishment. The person in your government, that is. They didn't spell it out, but they didn't have to. If I didn't obey, I'd be dead very soon."

"Without a name, I don't believe you, Vinke. Give me a name."

Captain Vinke removed his hat and brushed back the thinning white hair atop his head. "Can't do it, General. I'm sorry, but I can't do it."

"Think of your ship, Captain. I won't hesitate to sink you right now."

Vinke smiled and shook his head. "You don't have drones over my ship, General. I don't bluff as easily as my chief mate. To do that, you would have had to overfly sovereign territory and violate the air space of either Egypt or Saudi Arabia. I doubt either of them would approve of that."

"Unless I got their permission first."

"I'm still not buying it, Angriff. If I'm wrong, then aim for the bridge. I'll walk out on the port catwalk and wave to give you a better target."

Damn! Part of his brain had been clicking off the time while they spoke. Each second took the *Athena* farther from his stranded Zombies, and now Vinke had called his bluff. But even as he tried to think of how to get Vinke to change his mind, Fleming motioned him over and whispered in his ear.

"General, if we're done here, I need to prepare the ship for docking at Suez."

Angriff nodded at Fleming and came back into view of the computer's camera. "Do you have life insurance, Captain?"

"I told you I don't believe you."

"Why do you think you were ordered to leave those people behind, Vinke? C'mon, think about it; you're not a stupid man. Somebody doesn't want witnesses, so what does that make you?"

Now it was Vinke's turn to scowl in thought. "Witness to what?"

"To the identity of whoever called you, or those people you left behind, or the very existence of the

Athena, and who bankrolled her conversion... any or all of the above. Do you think it matters? Anybody who would go outside of the chain of command and order you to strand people you were contracted to pick up, knowing they would probably die, would think nothing of eliminating a ship's captain who knew their identity. You're a dead man walking, Vinke, unless you fulfill your contract with me."

Like a bunker-buster penetrating a hidey-hole the enemy thought was impervious, Angriff watched his salvo strike home with the captain.

The man's face sank into a deeper scowl. He blinked rapidly and pulled at his left eyebrow. "She would never do that," he muttered to himself, not meaning to say it loud enough for Angriff to hear.

But he did. *She.* That told Angriff everything he needed to know.

"Dozens of people are missing or buried who thought the same thing. You know I'm right, Captain. You know her track record. There are bodies all across the country. Your only chance of seeing next week is to let me protect you."

"You can do that? Against your own government?"

"I can and I will."

"How do I know you will keep your word?"

"There is nothing in this world I value more than my word of honor, Captain."

Vinke hesitated another ten seconds, and then turned to someone out of camera sight. "Bring us about, Mister de Haan. Steer one-seven-zero. Make for the rendevous point at fourteen knots."

"Fourteen knots, Captain?" came the response from de Haan, although Angriff couldn't see him.

"You heard me!"

0319 hours, October 1, 2012
The Red Sea east of the Egyptian coast
The five surfaced submarines rode a gentle swell twelve miles east of the compound, their engines off to conserve battery power. Salt spray ran down the glass canopies and reduced visibility in the dark night to less than one hundred yards, and the lapping of water was all they could hear. They were effectively deaf and blind, at the mercy of a pickup ship that was more than one hour late. And while he couldn't see them, Green Ghost had no doubt that Egyptian patrol craft were searching the waters surrounding the offshore compound for whoever had slaughtered Steyer and his hosts.

He opened the portside hatch and felt water droplets on his face. He'd hoped to hear better without the thick glass filtering out sounds, but if anything, it only magnified the splashing of the sea. Then he turned as Vapor touched his right shoulder.

"Wingnut needs a doctor soon, G.G. I think he's going into shock."

Apparently the inter-craft radio switch had been left on, because Adder chimed in within seconds. "Same goes for Frosty. She's lost a lot of blood."

"Roger that," he said, knowing there was nothing he could do. Plan B was desperate in the extreme, and only for those fit enough to hump it for days across a barren desert. Their wounded would never make it.

0401 hours, October 1, 2012
Bridge of the SS Athena
The instant Angriff signed off, Captain Vinke re-

duced speed to seven knots but stayed on the intercept course. With any luck, Angriff wouldn't notice the reduction until it was too late to pick up his people. It was a dangerous game, trying to convince both the American government and an angry combat general that he was following their contradictory orders, because Vinke had no doubt either one would be willing to order him killed. Unfortunately for him, Angriff had been expecting just such a move.

He had moved to the bridge wing when de Haan came out to get him again. "The general is back on the line, Captain, and he isn't happy."

"Kak!" he mouthed. *Shit!* He'd been caught.

"Flank speed, Mr. de Haan. Double the lookouts, and remind them we're looking for very small craft that look like glass eggs."

"Aye, sir."

Pushing away from the rail, he pulled a cigarette out of the pack, stuck it between his lips, and bent, lighting it between his hands. Drawing hard on the harsh Turkish tobacco, he blew out a lungful of smoke and then stepped inside to explain to Angriff how his engine room had misunderstood his orders to put on fourteen knots, but that had now been corrected. Vinke hoped like hell Angriff was as good as his word when it came to keeping him alive.

#

CHAPTER 14

"Never let the fear of striking out get in your way."
Babe Ruth

0426 hours, October 1, 2012
In the Red Sea

"Blue flare at ten o'clock."

Three hundred yards to port, a glowing circle of bluish-white arced across the sky before falling into the water. Green Ghost took off his headphones, picked up a flare gun brought along for just this purpose, leaned outside the open hatch, aimed it at a forty-five degree angle due east, and pulled the trigger. A red flare took seven seconds to carve its own trail through the darkness.

The ship that materialized on the black sea appeared huge beside the frail submarines, but in fact was only a medium-sized freighter streaked with rust. Written in block letters high on the bow was the name *Athena*. Slowing as it approached, the bow waves rocked the little undersea boats until the *Athena* coasted to a stop a few hundred yards to their right. Powering up the subs, the Zombies bobbed over the water at maximum topwater speed of eight knots. In the strong current, however, what should have taken five minutes took fifteen instead, so by the time they drew abeam the bridge, somebody was shouting at them with a bullhorn and a thick accent Green Ghost couldn't quite place.

"Hurry up and get your asses on board! The Egyptians are coming!"

He didn't waste time replying. Sitting back in the driver's seat, Green Ghost dogged the hatch and put on his headphones, flippling the intercom switch to *on.*

"Cia peb pib," he said in Hmong, the language of the reclusive Vietnamese hill people. It was the pre-arranged signal to start the recovery operation they had all practiced on the trip north, although never in a live drill. Anyone picking up their chatter was welcome to try and decipher it and, if they managed that, to figure out what special operations teams spoke Hmong. Using the foreign phrase also told his team that eavesdroppers might be nearby.

The first to submerge was Adder's, with the bad-ly wounded Frosty aboard. Once water covered the ship, they could follow its lights as it dove toward the *Athena's* center, where a blister identical to the one they'd used to exit from the *Roald Amundsen* was supposed to hang below the hull. The timetable called for the second submarine to follow after thirty seconds, and with Wingnut's leg wound still bleed-ing, Green Ghost put his own boat next in line.

The water level outside the glass canopy rose until it blotted out the night sky. Underwater was like being inside an oil spill, with the boat's head-lights projecting barely twenty feet forward before diffusing against a wall of blackness. The limited visibility left him to steer by depth and the homing beacon broadcast by the *Athena.* It wasn't much to go by. Without air conditioning he had to frequently blink sweat from his eyes.

The electric motors made a low humming sound as he increased RPMs to counteract the strong current that pushed the submarine sideways. His natural impulse was to creep forward, since the danger of slamming into the ship's hull was real. But every second Wingnut drew closer to bleeding out, so instead of throttling down Green Ghost increased speed.

There was a brief flash of red as *Athena's* bottom passed overhead. Then the dim outline of a lighted rectangle grew larger in the distance at eleven o'clock. He turned the wheel to the left and felt the submarine's stern begin to skid off to his right as the current threatened to send him spinning downstream. A fast glance showed the battery power below five percent, but there was no choice if Wingnut was going to have a chance. So he pushed the throttle all the way forward and prayed there was enough juice left to get them home.

Slowly, the boat moved forward against the current. The attitude was no longer ninety degrees to the waterlock entrance, but was closer to seventy degrees. Worse, off to his left Green Ghost saw the dim lights of the boat behind his. Unless he increased speed, they might collide. Even if they avoided a collision, there was no way he could wait and let them pass. Not only would he be risking Wingnut's life, but the batteries were too far gone for that.

His speed increased, and kept increasing, while at the same time the boat to his left kept coming. That was Judge's boat.

"You want me to call him?" Vapor said, unable to keep the tension out of his voice.

"No! We can't waste power on the radios."

Gripping the wheel like a race car driver, he

aimed for the lock, determined to get in. At the last second Judge slowed and backfilled, allowing him to pass into the water-filled area just as the RPMs started dropping. The batteries were empty. Not only did that mean no more engines, it also meant no more life support. Fortunately the subs were built with positive buoyancy, so the lack of power sent it floating to the surface.

Unlike the lock on the *Roald Amundsen*, which filled entirely with water once the submarines were manned, the one on *Athena* used pressurized air to allow for eight feet of breathable atmosphere so they could exit the subs. Through the heavy glass walls, Green Ghost saw four of the ship's crew operate hydraulic arms that gripped the submarine and held it on the starboard side, while a short steel ramp extended out to the portside hatch. To his right, on the opposite side of the lock, Adder and Nimcha lifted Frosty out and laid her on the steel deck. Then it was his and Vapor's turn to do the same thing with Wingnut.

One of the crewmen brought medical supplies in a large case and set them down beside the bleeding man and woman. Frosty's head lolled, but she was semi-conscious. Wingnut's pallid face showed no signs of life, although he was still breathing. Seconds later, a door opened in the far bulkhead and two men ran through, both wearing uniforms. Without a word the older of the two knelt beside Wingnut and began examining him, while the other took Green Ghost's arm. The specialized medical kits Green Ghost had requested lay within arm's reach.

"I am Chief Mate de Haan," he said, with the same accent as the man with the bullhorn. "Once all of your people are back, you must evacuate this pod immediately. An Egyptian missile boat is headed toward us at high speed and wants to board us, so you must be gone from here within five minutes."

Green Ghost didn't look up from Wingnut. He'd taken one round in the thigh and it must have nicked an artery. His skin was bleached with blood loss. "You want us *out* of here? Where are we supposed to go?"

"Yes, hurry! I'll show you the way."

"Why?"

"I'll explain later, but hurry for now."

With the imposition of such a short time limit, the docking of the other three submarines seemed painfully slow. Green Ghost and Vapor managed to stop Wingnut from bleeding using a combination of a combat tourniquet, copious amounts of hemostatic agent, and gauze, while Nimcha and Adder did the same thing for Frosty. The rest of the Zombies assembled two stretchers from the medical kits, gently laid their fallen comrades on the tightly woven mesh, and followed de Haan from the chamber and up a series of ladders to the ship's sick bay.

Green Ghost leaned against the bulkhead as his team filed out. Dirt and blood spattered his uniform. When Adder walked by, he held up a hand to stop the man; it was time to forge a bond.

"You did a helluva job out there," he said.

"Thanks. And you weren't the worst team leader I've ever had."

Green Ghost's face betrayed no reaction. It was a look the Zombies would come to know well in the coming years, but for now, it was new and unknown.

"Don't lay it on so thick," he finally said.

Adder winked.

Sickbay was a long, narrow room with three examination tables lined up end to end on a blue linoleum floor. White walls reflected bright overhead fluorescent lights amid a maze of wires, conduits, and machines. The *Athena's* doctor, a stocky man named Pietr Van Graan, wore a white smock with a large red cross on front and back. He had already given Wingnut a cursory exam and concluded that he could do nothing more aboard ship than Green Ghost and Vapor had already done, except give plasma to keep the wounded man's blood volume up.

Frosty was a different story. The on-duty nurse, a stout blonde with a suspicious glare and a matching smock to Van Graan's, stood ready to assist the doctor. A blazing exam lamp bent close to her face, picking out every detail as the doctor's eyes inspected the wound in her cheek. With Adder and Green Ghost at his elbow, he said nothing, but instead issued a steady stream of grunts. Then, without warning, the ship lurched and a loud *chunk* echoed throughout the hull.

"What the fuck was that?" cried several Zombies at the same time.

The nurse glanced at them as if a buffalo had left behind a manure pile. She actually sneered as she replied. "Ons het waarskynlik pod die pod vrygestel." *They probably released the pod.*

Adder responded within seconds. "Praat u nie Engels nie?" *Do you not speak English?*

She leaned back as if slapped. Blue eyes went wide and the slightest trace of a smile cracked her lips. Before answering, she looked him up and down like a gourmet ogling a three-star meal. "You speak Afrikaans?" She had less of an accent than either the doctor or de Haan.

"Dit is duidelik dat." *Obviously.*

"You wanna clue the rest of us in?" said Green Ghost. "Unless you're lining up a date for later."

"They jettisoned that pod we came in through."

"Why would they do that?" asked Vapor.

Green Ghost didn't need anyone else to answer that question. "In case the Egyptians send down divers."

0723 hours, October 3, 2012
Camp Zippo, Djibouti

Nick Angriff's favorite accoutrement at Camp Zippo was the ice machine. It had been hard not only to find one, but also to get it hooked up properly in the middle of the desert. But it had been oh, so worth it! Since there was no local water source, that meant using water brought in by trucks and pumped into the elaborate plumbing system of the four interconnected modules serving the 200-odd personnel who made up the camp's staff. As for the general who had personally chosen its isolated location and made his office there, he plucked two cubes out of the ice machine's well and dropped them into a cup of steaming black coffee.

As he passed through the tiny common area on the way to his office, the *majordomo* of his headquarters, E-7 Mandel, spotted him and jumped up, eyebrows raised. "I'm sorry, General. I could have gotten that for you."

"I'm not a cripple, Emily." He glanced at the old-style clock on the wall. "Besides, you don't go on duty until oh-eight hundred. Me having to get my own coffee won't show up on your EPR."

Mandel still didn't look happy and Angriff knew why. She considered the office as her personal responsibility, him included, and wanted everything to run in perfect coordination. It was what made her indispensable in his eyes. Angriff had taken four steps toward his office door at the far end of a narrow hallway when Mandel's voice came from behind him.

"General Steeple on the secure video line, sir."

Angriff half-turned. "Steeple?" He paused and absorbed the info. "Thank you, Emily. I'll take it from here. Oh, before I forget... remind me to authorize a new patch."

"Should I also remind you who it's for, General?"

"No need, I'll know."

Settling into his favorite desk chair, the one missing its left arm, Angriff sipped his coffee and then clicked a flashing red light on the bottom toolbar of his computer monitor to join the video conference. General Thomas Francis Steeple's thin face fuzzed into view and, while Angriff didn't know him well, he thought the man looked thinner and more careworn than in their previous call.

"Sorry to keep you waiting, General Steeple," he said, being purposefully formal. "I know this must be important; it's what, past midnight where you are?"

"It's all right, Nick. Remember, first names?"

"All right... Tom." Something didn't sound right in Angriff's ear, some inner instinct warning him to be wary of this man, but what could he do? Not calling him by his first name could be viewed as an insult, and Angriff wasn't so without ambition that he wanted to piss off the most powerful man in the U.S. Army.

"Good... I've had a long day, Nick, so let me get

right to the point. You angered some people this week, powerful people who would not mind seeing you replaced as USAC Commander."

"Is that what this call is? Am I relieved of my command?"

"No! Hell, no. And as long as I'm CJCS," he pronounced each letter, C-J-C-S, "you will remain at your post. I just thought you needed to know where you stood with certain higher-ups."

"In that case, thank you, Tom. I appreciate your support."

"You're welcome. But do me one favor, Nick… try not to make any more enemies for a while. I've gotten quite an earful the last two days."

Angriff smiled, but it didn't reflect his inner mood. There was just something about Steeple he didn't trust. They didn't know each other very well, yet apparently Steeple had gone to bat for him and saved his job. *Why?* "I'll try not to anger anybody without need, Tom."

"Thank you, Nick. Your country needs you now, and in the future. Maybe even the far future."

"I don't follow."

This time it was Steeple's turn to smile. "We'll talk about that when the time comes."

The End

If you enjoyed this story, please leave a review at Amazon, Goodreads, or on your favorite message board. For more information on William Alan Webb and the world of The Last Brigade, please visit his website at www.thelastbrigade.com

ABOUT THE AUTHOR

He's the world's oldest teenager. Reading, writing, and rock & roll make for an awesome life. The occasional beach doesn't hurt, either.

Bill grew up in West Tennessee, riding his bike on narrow rural roads lined with wild blackberry bushes, in the days before urban sprawl. He spent those long rides dreaming of new worlds of adventure. Childhood for him was one interesting activity after another, from front yard football to naval miniatures, but from the very beginning reading was the central pillar of his life.

Any and all military history books fascinated him, beginning before age eight. By his teenage years, he had discovered J.R.R. Tolkien and Robert E. Howard, Robert Heinlein and Fritz Leiber. Teachers ripped comic books out of his hands during Spanish and accounting classes. Oops!

College found him searching for his favorite rock groups, smuggling beer into his dorm room, and growing his hair long. He read a book a day back then, sometimes two, and always SFF. He even went to class sometimes.

After college, he turned to writing history and nonfiction and was published a number of times, including in *World War Two* magazine.

In September of 2014, he wrote the first pages of

what would become *Standing The Final Watch* and its direct sequel, *Standing In The Storm*, plus the fill-in work *The Ghost of Voodoo Village*. That was followed in 2017 by the launch of a brand new fantasy series **Sharp Steel and High Adventure**, starting with the novella *Two Moons Waning*. Who says you can't teach an old dog new tricks? And if you like his work, a whole slew of new books are on the schedule for 2019 and 2020.

Bill is an Active (voting) member of the Science Fiction & Fantasy Writers of America, the Society For Military History, and the Alliance of Independent Authors. He writes exclusive stories for those on his mailing list at his website, www.thelastbrigade.com.

In at the Start
a story set in the world of
The Last Brigade

June 23, 1995

The blue intercom light blinked and General Isaac Ismay shook his head in frustration. "We're never going to get through this," he said, giving Colonel Tom Steeple his most exasperated look. Steeple nodded, and was very glad he wasn't the cause of the general's displeasure.

Ismay pushed the blue button.

"General, a Mister Roger Deeson from NASA is here to see you."

"NASA? What's he want with Personnel?"

"I don't know, General, but he says it's urgent."

"It always is." Steeple knew what was coming next. Clicking off the intercom, Ismay gave a dismissive wave. "Get rid of him, Tom, but hurry. If we don't have these new OER standards in place by Friday, Shalishkavili will have my ass. And they've got to conform to Zero Defect."

"Yes, sir," Steeple said. Outwardly he appeared calm, but inside he seethed. He'd been trying to get his boss to work on the OER updates for four months. Now, when he couldn't put it off any longer, it suddenly became urgent, so whatever this Deeson guy wanted, it'd better be quick.

Roger Deeson rose as Steeple came through the side door to the front waiting room. Steeple saw the faces of the other hopefuls waiting to see the general, who obviously wondered why a man who had just walked in rated an immediate audience with his adjutant. After shaking hands, Steeple led Deeson through a warren of cubicles to his own small office. A corporal asked if they needed anything and Steeple shook his head; this wouldn't last that long.

"Do I understand correctly that you're from NASA, Mr. Deeson?"

"Yes, Colonel, yes, that's right. I'm here on a matter of... of..." He fumbled for the words and pulled at his lower lip.

"It's all right, Mr. Deeson, please don't be nervous. Just tell me how I can help you."

"I need to see the general right away... it's a matter of national security."

"I'm afraid that's not possible. The general is tied up on a Personnel matter of the highest importance, and I doubt he'll be available for an extended period. Weeks, at the least. Perhaps I can help you, if you explain to me why you wish to see the general."

"I've heard that a lot in the past few days."

"I beg your pardon?"

Deeson sucked a noisy breath through his nose. "You're not my first choice for divulging this information to, Colonel. No offense, but I've tried every office of every branch before I came to you. You are, literally, my last hope."

"I see. So you weren't seeking the help of the Personnel Department specifically?"

"No." He lowered his head in shame at being forced to admit this. "But then, perhaps this is for the best. Now that I think about it, Personnel might be the perfect partner to get this off the ground."

"Get what off the ground, Mister Deeson? Please, just tell my why you're here."

Deeson blurted his message. "If you knew the country was doomed, what would you be willing to do to stop it?"

"Doomed?" Steeple nodded, as though he understood, whereas he really wondered how such a nutcase had been allowed into the Pentagon. Still, it was always a good idea to remain polite when dealing with representatives of other government agencies. "By doomed, do you mean that we are all going to die eventually?"

"No, no, that's not what I mean at all." Deeson paused and swallowed. "May I have some water?"

Steeple smiled, although he really wanted this strange man to leave so he could get back to work. He buzzed his administrative assistant and after the corporal brought them both a glass of water, Deeson downed his and appeared more composed.

"Thank you. And thank you for not throwing me out yet, for at least hearing what I have to say. I realize how I must sound to you. You're the first to let me get this far and I appreciate your open-mindedness. I can assure you, Colonel, I'm not a crank. I hold a PhD in computer science and programming from Penn, the University of Pennsylvania, and am considered the world's leading expert on predictive and actuarial programming. You can look that up if you like. I have a copy of my biography in my briefcase."

"Thank you, uh, Doctor Deeson, but that won't

be necessary. You sound very qualified in your field of... what is it exactly that you do?"

"I program computers to make predictions, mostly for NASA, occasionally for other government agencies."

In Steeple's mind he snapped his fingers. *Aha,* he thought. *Other agencies; that's how he got into the Pentagon.*

"What I'm going to tell you now," Deeson said, "is strictly confidential. You may, of course, share it with whomever you think it wise, and of course with General Ismay, but if it got out to the general public there could be a panic."

"I think I know how to keep a secret, Doctor. You said we're doomed; what did you mean?"

A change came over Deeson's lean face. Instead of the socially awkward introvert who first sat down, his expression became that of a confident teacher in a room full of students.

"Most celestial bodies in our solar system are pockmarked with craters. These are from past impacts by objects such as asteroids. Earth is no different, except water hides many of the impact craters. These events have ranged from minor strikes by golfball-sized meteorites, which lost most of their mass burning through our atmosphere, to the comet that ended the Cretaceous period and wiped out the dinosaurs. The Permian Extinction two hundred fifty million years ago wiped out ninety-six percent of marine life on Earth. Think about that, Colonel — our seas became virtually sterile. Seventy percent of terrestrial vertebrates died out. Earth was largely devoid of higher species and it took tens of millions of years for the planet to recover... and once the dinosaurs had covered the globe, another comet destroyed them."

"Are you telling me a comet is headed for Earth?" Steeple said, at once alarmed and confused. If that were true, why tell him? Why wasn't NASA scrambling for an answer?

"Oh, no, Colonel... at least, not that I'm aware of. But you see, NASA knows we might not have much warning even if such an event were imminent. Asteroids tend to be invisible with our current technology until very close to Earth. But it *is* possible such a danger is out there, and given the data on past events, I'm able to write a program to predict the probabilities for such a future event."

"So the probability is high?" Despite himself, Steeple was becoming interested.

"No, Colonel, just the opposite. It's remote."

"I—" Steeple paused. Burgeoning interest had become impatience. "Doctor, forgive me being so blunt, but could you please come to the point? I doubt you're here to warn the Personnel Department of the United States Army that a remote chance exists of an asteroid striking Earth and wiping out all life on the planet."

"In a roundabout way, yes, I am. But bear with me just a moment longer. *Please.* Do you believe there could ever be a nuclear war, Colonel?"

"Yes, of course I do."

"What about a pandemic? A deadly new flu variant, or maybe an AIDS-like virus that spreads through the air? Ebola, perhaps. The Black Death wiped out a third of Europe's population; do you think such a thing could happen again?"

"I don't know, maybe. Medicine has come a long way since the fourteenth century."

"And yet we cannot cure the common cold."

131

"Doctor, *please get to the point!*"

"In the course of my work, I wrote a program for NASA to predict the chances of a catastrophic event overtaking the United States. When the results came back, the NASA leadership ordered them sealed. I was forbidden to disclose what they concluded. By speaking to you today, I'm technically committing a felony, although I'm not worried about prison. To prosecute me, they would have to bring other agencies into the loop on what I found, agencies over which they have no control…"

"The point, Doctor Deeson?"

"The point, Colonel, is that we face many, many dire threats, any one of which could destroy our country. No single threat scores very high on the probability curve, but taken all together they predict a ninety-seven point seven three percent chance of the United States facing catastrophic collapse within the next fifty years. Something is going to kill us, Colonel; we just don't know what it will be."

Steeple leaned back and pulled at his ear. It was the *tell* that kept him from winning at poker and showed he was thinking about the man's words. He said nothing for nearly thirty seconds, merely staring at the man seated in front of his desk.

Finally, he sat up straight. "As I see it, you're either a raving lunatic, or a man bearing the most important message this building may have heard. Quite obviously my fellow officers concluded the former, but I pride myself on reading people, on knowing who's competent and who's not. So before I make up my mind, answer me this… so what?"

"I beg your pardon?"

"So what? Let's say you're right; what can we do about it? How can we prepare for a disaster when we don't know what it will be or when it will happen? But let's say I believe you, Doctor Deeson, that I'm sold, lock, stock, and barrel. I'm a colonel in a building full of generals. What do you think I can do?"

"Convince General Ismay to hear me out."

"Doctor, believe me when I tell you that won't happen unless the president orders him to listen. General Ismay has other concerns." *Like the brunette in the condo he pays for,* he thought.

"But... but the fate of the country is at stake! Maybe the world!"

"The less you say that, the better. I'm afraid you come off as histrionic, if not unbalanced."

"I know I sound like a nut." Deeson dropped his head. "I've been told it often enough. It's just that... oh, hell, what's the use?"

"Surely NASA knows to take this seriously?"

"NASA has their head in the sand... no, not in the sand, up their own ass. Colonel, if you don't help me, I don't know where to turn next. I have the most important warning our country has ever received and no one will heed it. It's like those cryptographers trying to warn their superiors about Pearl Harbor, but nobody would listen."

"I would like to help you, Doctor Deeson, but I don't see how I can."

"Would you at least meet one of my colleagues? Perhaps she can convince you that we deserve your support?"

"And who might that be?"

"What are your dinner plans, Colonel?"

Steeple loved fine dining. The rituals of proper

service, combined with fine table cloths and exquis-
ite accoutrements, appealed to his penchant for or-
derliness and structure.

Grimaldi's Italian Kitchen was none of that. To
his way of thinking, it was scarcely above a dive,
with poor lighting and red and white plastic table
covers. The silverware might or might not have been
clean; he couldn't tell because the finish was too
worn away. It was the type of place he would never
frequent by choice.

Grimaldi's was small, just four booths along one
wall and five tables nearby. He'd sat at the last
booth as instructed, and realized with surprise why
Deeson had chosen this place — anybody trying to
listen in would be obvious, since he was the sole
customer.

Less than five minutes after Steeple sat down,
Deeson came in, preceded by a small, frail-looking
woman of indeterminate age.

"Colonel Thomas Steeple," Deeson said, "allow
me to introduce Doctor Siree Shankur."

Aside from her Indian ancestry and the bindi on
her forehead, Shankur's most striking feature was
the fire in her brown eyes. Steeple had rarely felt an
aura of power such as she projected. From such a
diminutive woman, it was startling.

After an exchange of pleasantries, Shankur got
right to the point. "How open-minded are you, Colonel Steeple?" Only a trace remained of an accent;
otherwise she sounded like anyone else from the
American Midwest.

"That depends on the subject, Doctor. In some
ways I'm very open-minded; in others, not so much.
Could you be a little more specific?"

A heavy-set waitress interrupted to ask if they

wanted anything. Steeple ordered Scotch, no ice, but accepted a Peroni beer when informed beer was the only alcohol they served. She asked if he wanted a glass and he said no. *Who knows the last time they washed it?* Deeson and Shankur asked for water.

"Scientifically speaking," she said. "What if you were shown a new technology that most would write off as science fiction, but was real? Could you accept such a fact?"

"If we're speaking theoretically, how could I not?"

"So you're not the suspicious sort?"

"I didn't say that. People are always playing fast and loose with the truth to advance their agenda, so I expect it. But if I'm presented with facts, how can I not believe them?"

"How indeed? Yet others have said that and then, when confronted with evidence contradictory to their ingrained beliefs, denied the proof of their own eyes."

"Doctor, I'm a realist. If something exists, then it exists. But that also makes me a skeptic. You first have to prove to me the something in question really does exist."

"Very well," she said with a nod. "At this juncture I can ask for nothing more." Turning to Roger, she nodded again.

He immediately took up the narrative. "Earlier today, I asked you a question you didn't answer, so I'd like to ask it again. If you knew, beyond the shadow of a doubt, that the United States was doomed, what would you be willing to do to prevent that, or to at least mitigate the damage?"

"I've been in the United States Army for nearly twenty years. I have literally given my life for this country, so the answer to your question is I would do anything to save it."

"Anything, Colonel?"

"*Anything*, Doctor."

"That's easy to say, sitting in a restaurant sipping a drink. If you say yes to what we're going to propose, I hope in the years to come you remember you said that." Deeson turned back to Shankur, her cue to take over.

"Tell me, Colonel," she said. "What do you know about cryogenics?"

Steeple sat for half an hour after they left. His Peroni sat untouched; his meal of manicotti with meat sauce had gone cold on the plate. When the restaurant door opened, he didn't notice. Soft footfalls on the tile floor also went unheard.

When a stocky man in an overcoat pulled out a chair and sat where Shankur had been seated, Steeple didn't act surprised. "FBI?" he said. "Army CID? NSA?"

"Something like that," the newcomer said.

"Do I get a name, or does this happen like in the movies where the mysterious stranger refuses to identify himself?"

"Wesley Dunn," he said. Leaning forward, he pushed away the remnants of Shankur's meal and used a clean knife to cut off a corner of Steeple's manicotti. Using his fingers, he popped it into his mouth and nodded approval. "Not bad, considering it's cold."

"You're welcome to it."

"Nah, thanks, my girlfriend put my dinner in the oven to keep it warm."

"So, are we done here?"

Dunn grinned. "I knew I was going to like you. So what did Doctor Doomsday tell you?"

"You're not FBI," Steeple said, studying the fleshy face across the table. "Those guys have no sense of humor and are circumspect about everything. Definitely not ACID, either. NSA is out, too."

"Why is that?" Dunn seemed to be enjoying himself.

"They're way above my pay grade. That only leaves one possibility... the Company."

"You really should try the manicotti. I've had better, but not a lot better. Looks like she had seafood ravioli. I'll bet it was tasty."

After studying his face for a few seconds, Steeple pointed at him. "You don't know her name. You're hoping I'll drop it in idle conversation."

Dunn shrugged. "You're a smart man, Colonel, but she's not that important... So, like I said, my girlfriend's waiting for me, so we can keep playing footsie or we can cut to the chase. I don't care either way. My girlfriend's a lousy cook."

"Doctor Doomsday, huh? So what's his story?"

"Roger Deeson is a brilliant computer programmer. I daresay there's nobody better, particularly when it comes to risk assessment. However, his genius lies in interpreting facts and correlating statistics, not in predicting the future. He deals in probabilities based on..." Dunn paused and raised a finger. "And this is key... probabilities based on *factual data*. As long as he has reliable data to work with, his conclusions are trustworthy. Unfortunately, he used what is tantamount to guesswork in this doomsday model of his. The conclusion is invalid because the input data was invalid."

"I see. And you're telling me this because...?"

"You're one of the young turks of the army; your career is flagged for special attention. We both know you're ambitious, Colonel, and that you're aiming for the top. I'd hate to see your career derailed by a deluded man's fear-driven fantasy."

"All I've done so far is listen and ask questions."

"Just be sure that a listening ear doesn't become a running mouth."

"I'm disappointed. I thought we were friends. I even shared my manicotti with you."

Dunn wiped his mouth and stood. "I like you, Colonel. Don't do anything stupid."

"I never do."

Holding his broad umbrella tight in the wind, Steeple avoided puddles in the parking lot, but the driving rain soaked his shoes anyway. Once in his car, he locked the doors and wondered if it was bugged. He often spoke to himself while driving, talking out scenarios of whatever problems he faced at the time, but now he kept quiet, in case someone was listening. Crossing the Potomac into Arlington, he pulled over at the first lighted phone booth he saw.

He didn't call Deeson, whose phone was probably bugged. Instead he called Siree Shankur.

"I'm taking you up on your offer," he said. "Show me these frozen people."

To be continued...

The shouts of battle faded as the men who made them cried and died. Echoes of steel on steel disappeared into the murky depths of the deep valley, below steep slopes, and the carnage of war lay scattered across snow-clad fields. The copper scent of blood tainted the wind. Here and there, frozen hands reached skyward, as if in supplication to their gods.

The bearskin-clad bodies of the Vorge war party lay in heaps around the corpses of four Yetondi, the race of white-furred giants who lived in the high mountains along the northern border of Corland. The Yetondi had stolen Vorge livestock and such thievery couldn't go unanswered. Of the thirty Vorge who'd trudged into the mountains three days earlier, and the six Yetondi who'd intercepted them, only two of each fought on.

A distant screech went unheard by the remaining combatants. Alden Havenwulf heard only the crunch of his boots breaking through the ice layer that covered the snow, and the grunts of his massive opponent.

"Dexter, do you live?" he shouted, without taking his eyes off the monster in front of him. Alden danced with the grace of an experienced swordsman, keeping the Yetondi out of reach while not daring to turn around. His voice echoed down the wind.

"I'm having sport with this one," came the hoarse reply.

The two Yetondi whooped and stomped the snow, baring yellowed tusks as they screamed in rage. Despite their monstrous appearance, Alden knew the Yetondi were intelligent creatures. When the one facing him roared in fury for his fallen tribesmen, Alden felt himself tremble. Then the huge mouth formed sounds it was never meant to form.

"You die for killing Grishnah," the Yetondi said in Corlandish. The words sounded like a cross between the roar of a bear and a man speaking underwater. At the end, he whooped, as if punctuating his words.

"One of us dies today," Alden said. "Let's find out which one."

The last four combatants parried and thrust in two separate fights to the death. Hard panting seared the humans' lungs as they gulped in the freezing air. The bitter atmosphere did not bother the Yetondi, who had adapted to the harsh conditions over a thousand generations. Nine feet tall and protected by thick white fur, the manlike apes were in their natural environment.

At such a high altitude, the bleak sun glittered in silver on the frozen fields. The men had to protect their eyes from the burning reflections, but the Yetondi had developed a thick membrane to filter out sunlight that might burn their retinas.

As they circled and feinted, using up precious energy, the bitter conditions took their toll. Feeling his strength waning and his movements slowing, Alden knew he had to win the fight soon, if he was going to win at all.

He maneuvered so the huge creature blocked out the sun as it towered over him. Thick lips drew back over fangs half a foot long. It snarled something in its language and began to swing a huge, multi-pointed axe around its head. Watching it whirl faster and faster, Alden knew that standing still meant death. Yet he felt his muscles tighten with fatigue, and knew that sooner or later he would move a second too slow. A desperate plan came to mind, gambling his own superhuman Corlandish reflexes against the speed of the axe.

He pretended to slip and struggle for balance. Without warning, the axe whistled downward at Alden's head, accelerating with enough force to split him in two. But he had expected just such a blow. With scant inches to spare he jumped left, rolled to his feet in the knee-high snow, and thrust upward, aiming for his huge opponent's ribcage.

A lesser blade wouldn't have penetrated the layered skins and hard leather jerkin beneath, but Alden's rapier slid into the giant's chest. He had aimed for a fatal blow into the lungs, but the beast only staggered before regaining his footing.

Enraged and fueled by pain, the Yetondi's axe whistled as he swung it backhand. Alden threw himself face-first in the snow. He tried to roll over but the deep powder held him tight. Legs apart, the Yetondi lifted its axe high overhead. Alden twisted his head to watch his doom. Glistening in the sun, the axe's head loomed against the sky as the Yetondi raised it for the death blow. This time Alden knew he couldn't avoid it.

But sunlight also picked out a spreading crimson stain on the Yetondi's chest. Holding the axe at its apex, the Yetondi coughed and staggered backward as blood bubbled from his mouth. He dropped the weapon in a high drift and fell to his knees, wheezing. Opening the skins and jerkin, the creature touched the bloody fur on his chest and met Alden's gaze. The Corlandishman saw disbelief mixed with agony reflected in the large brown eyes. The Yetondi realized death was near. When the two combatants locked gazes again, Alden knew he had slain a man.

In a fit of twitching, the Yetondi toppled forward. Hot blood melted the snow around him.

#

Also by William Alan Webb

The Last Brigade — Books
Standing The Final Watch
The Ghost of Voodoo Village: Short Story and Bonus Chapters for Standing The Final Watch
Standing In The Storm
Standing At The Edge
Standing Before Hell's Gate
Standing With Righteous Rage (coming early 2020)
Standing Among The Tombstones (coming late 2020)

The Last Brigade — Stories
The Hairy Man – Winner 2019 Imadjinn Award, Finalist 2019 Darrell Award
The River of Walking Spirits — (Coming early 2020)
In At The Start — (Coming 2020)

Task Force Zombie
The Nameless
Not Enough Bullets — (Coming 2020)

Time Wars – Books
Jurassic Jail — Finalist for 2019 Imadjinn Award
Cretaceous Kill — with J. Gunnar Grey (Coming early 2020)
Dark Time — (Coming late 2020)

Time Wars – Stories
Tail Gunner Joe

Sharp Steel & High Adventure
Two Moons Waning
The Queen of Death and Darkness
A Night at the Quay — Winner of the 2018 Darrell Award
Sharp Steel — (Collection)
The Demon in the Jewel — (Coming 2020)
Beyond the Dead River — (Coming early 2020)
The Dragons of Anthar — (Coming late 2020)

Hit World
Kill Me When You Can
Shoot First — with Larry Hoy
Kill Me If You Will (Coming 2020)

Other Stories
Grinning Soul — with Thomas Lyon Russell
The Granite Man, The Dream Realms of Cthulu — (Coming late 2019)
The Moles of Vienna — (Coming early 2020)
The Sting of Fate — (Coming Dec. 2019)
Hitler a la Mode — (Coming 2020)

Non-Fiction
The Last Attack: Sixth SS Panzer Army and the Defense of Hungary and Austria, 1945
Killing Hitler's Reich, The Battle for Austria, 1945
Killing Hitler's Reich, The Battle for Velikiye Luki, 1942-1943 — (Coming 2020)
Unsuck Your Book, 8 Months From First Draft to the Promised Land
Unsuck Your Book Career, What I've Learned — (Coming 2020)

Thanks for reading! Dingbat Publishing strives to bring you quality entertainment that doesn't take itself too seriously. I mean honestly, with a name like that, our books have to be good or we're going to be laughed at. Or maybe both.

If you enjoyed this book, the best thing you can do is buy a million more copies and give them to all your friends... erm, leave a review on the readers' website of your preference. All authors love feedback and we take reviews from readers like you seriously.

Oh, and c'mon over to our website:
www.DingbatPublishing.ninja

Who knows what other books you'll find there?

Cheers,

Gunnar Grey,
publisher, author, and Chief Dingbat

δ

Made in the USA
Coppell, TX
04 September 2021

61774535R00085